A Daring Plan

Brittany reached into her closet for a sweater. Her hand went automatically to a plain navy blue one, but then the raspberry-colored cardigan her mother had been admiring caught her eye. She took it off the hanger and slipped it over her shoulders, seeing herself reflected in the mirror on the opposite wall.

Her mother was right. The sweater did look beautiful on her. Brittany shook out her hair so that it fell in shining blond waves over her shoulders. Beautiful Brittany. That's what people had been saying about her all her life. Usually she hated those words. They made her wish she was invisible. But now, for the first time, she hoped they were true. Because her entire project—maybe the fate of the whole club—depended on them!

Beautiful Brittany

Beautiful Brittany

Susan Meyers

little rainbow®
Troll Associates

Beautiful Brittany

Brittany Logan opened her eyes. Everything was quiet—so quiet that for a moment she wasn't sure where she was. No taxis honked outside her window, no buses lumbered past, no sirens howled in the distance. She turned over beneath her blue-and-white-striped comforter. Her pale yellow, lace-trimmed nightgown twisted around her knees. Her long tawny blond hair tumbled over the pillow.

Brittany closed her eyes for a moment, still caught between sleeping and waking, then opened them again to see a pool of sunlight falling on the polished hardwood floor by her bed. A blue jay, landing on the pine tree outside her window, squawked loudly, cocked its head, and eyed her warily through the glass.

And all at once she remembered.

Redwood Grove—that's where she was! Not in the Logans' penthouse apartment high above the traffic-choked streets of New York, not in their high-ceilinged flat off a busy boulevard in Paris, France, not in Switzerland where she'd attended boarding school last year. No. She was here, in her very own sunlight-filled room in their house high in the tree-covered hills above the town of Redwood Grove, California, just across the bay from San Francisco. Her home, now and forever she hoped.

She threw back the covers and sat up, startling the jay, which flapped away in a whirl of blue feathers.

"Ah! You're awake." Brittany's mother poked her head around the door. "I was just coming to get you. You'll be late for your meeting if you don't get up soon."

"Oh no! What time is it?" cried Brittany. Rubbing the sleep out of her blue eyes, which were fringed with long dark lashes, she stared disbelievingly at her night table clock. The red numbers flashed 10:05. And the club meeting—the very first meeting of the Always Friends Club that she was in charge of, the meeting at which she would present her plan for a project that she hoped would keep the club from falling apart—was scheduled to begin at eleven. How could she have slept so long?

"You must have been tired," said Mrs. Logan, opening the door all the way and stepping into the room. She was a famous fashion designer, and as always, she was beautifully dressed. The loose-fitting jacket, silk blouse, and slacks that she was wearing were from her own fall collection. "But don't worry," she added, smiling. "You have plenty of time. *Beaucoup de temps*," she repeated in French, which both she and Brittany spoke fluently. "All you have to do is get dressed. Now let's see . . ."

She swept across the room to the closet, which took up an entire wall, and slid open the doors. Like all the closets in the house, it had been planned by a professional designer. Everything had its own special place. Blouses and skirts, jackets and dresses, hung neatly from white metal rods fixed at varying heights from the floor. Sweaters, blue jeans, and T-shirts were stacked in sliding metal baskets. Scarves and belts hung from hooks, and shoes and boots were arranged on racks, while socks, underwear, and nightclothes were tucked away neatly in drawers.

It was all incredibly orderly. *And* embarrassing, Brittany thought now, remembering the way her friends' closets looked. Luckily, today's meeting was being held in town at Elmer's Ice Cream Emporium, not at her house, so she wouldn't have to worry about keeping the door shut to hide all that neatness. But she would have to choose her own outfit to wear. Otherwise she'd wind up in a silk blouse and cashmere sweater while everyone else was in T-shirts and jeans.

"You don't have to pick out anything for me, Mom," she said, jumping out of bed and rushing to the closet. The shaggy white throw rug on the floor felt warm and familiar beneath her bare feet. But the word *mom* felt strange coming out of her mouth. Until moving to Redwood Grove a few months ago, she'd always called her parents "Mother" and "Father," not "Mom" and "Dad." But she was determined to change. She was determined to talk and dress just like any other ten-year-old girl in town. Especially to dress like one. "I'll just wear these," she said, snatching a pair of jeans and a plain white T-shirt from one of the sliding metal baskets.

"Oh, but don't you think . . ." Mrs. Logan began, her hand lingering over a raspberry-colored cable-knit cardigan. "This is such a wonderful color on you and it would go beautifully with—But wait. What am I doing?" She held up her hands as if to surrender and backed away from the closet. "Sorry, Brittany," she said. "I just can't seem to get it through my head that you don't need me to choose your clothes anymore."

"That's okay, Mom," said Brittany quickly, the *mom* coming more easily this time. She wished she hadn't been in such a hurry to rush to the closet. She hadn't meant to hurt her mother's feelings. She knew how hard she was trying.

"No, it's not okay," said Mrs. Logan. "I promised you when we moved here that we were going to make some changes in our lives, and this is one of them. I hereby pledge that I will not look in this closet again. You don't need me dressing you up like some kind of fashion doll. You can choose your own clothes, and when they're dirty you can dump them on the closet floor and shut the door like girls your age usually do, and I won't even know it!"

Brittany laughed. She couldn't help it. Her mother sounded so earnest. "Oh, Mother! I mean, Mom," she corrected herself. "You know I couldn't do that. I'm as much of a neatness freak as you are. I just don't want my friends to know it."

"Well, I certainly won't tell," said Mrs. Logan, laughing. "It'll be our secret—neatness freaks united!" She gave Brittany a quick hug. "Now get yourself dressed. I'll drive you to town on my way to San Francisco, and then pick you up later at Meg's house. I wish you could have had your friends here for the meeting, but I've been wanting to have lunch with Kiki Johnson and this was the only time she had free. She's been incredibly busy lately."

The mention of Kiki Johnson, Mrs. Logan's old friend from design school, who was now the owner of a children's clothing company called Kiki for Kids, made Brittany forget about neat closets and what she should wear. Kiki—Aunt Kiki, as Brittany had always called her—was important. *Very* important. In fact, Brittany's entire scheme, everything she planned to set in motion at the club meeting today, depended on her. "I hope she's not going to be too busy to come to your party," she said anxiously.

"Don't worry about that," Mrs. Logan replied. "She wouldn't miss it for the world. If I know Kiki, she'll be the first to arrive and the last to leave. She loves a good party, and she's eager to see you again, too, Brittany. Every time I talk to her she asks, 'How's my beautiful Brittany?' I think she's still hoping you'll agree to appear in one of her catalogs, though I keep telling her you don't want to have anything to do with modeling."

"Well, that may not be exactly—" Brittany began, but Mrs. Logan wasn't listening. Her eyes had fallen on the clock by Brittany's bed.

"Oh, look at the time!" she exclaimed. "I'd better go make a few phone calls before we leave. I need to reschedule things so I'll have plenty of time Monday afternoon to measure your friends for their costumes. Flower Fairies! Such a wonderful idea. It'll absolutely make the party!" She gave Brittany another quick squeeze, then swept out of the room, leaving only the familiar scent of her favorite perfume behind.

Brittany took a deep breath. Sometimes being around her mother made her feel like she'd been in the presence of a whirlwind. She was so full of energy and enthusiasm. Even now, after they'd moved to Redwood Grove in order to lead a simpler life, after she'd handed most of the day-to-day management of her company over to others, she still seemed as busy as ever. She was designing clothes for her next collection, setting up a San Francisco office, decorating the new house, giving parties . . . and now she was ready to transform Brittany and her friends into flowers—or rather, into Flower Fairies.

Forgetting for a moment about getting dressed, Brittany sat down on her bed and picked up the small picture book lying beside the clock on her night table. *Flower Fairies of the Summer* by Cicely Mary Barker. She opened the cover and leafed through the pages of delicate watercolor paintings of Flower Fairies— creatures that looked like children with wings sprouting out of their backs dressed in costumes made of flower petals. There were poems, too, but they were sort of icky. It was the pictures that Brittany loved.

She'd found the little volume buried in a bin of old books in a musty-smelling used bookstore in England where she and her parents were vacationing. It had been published a long time ago and she'd never seen another like it, which made it all the more special. Her father had bought the book for her. She'd taken it with her to boarding school last year and it had helped her get through some difficult times. She'd often fallen asleep in her dormitory at night looking at the illustrations and imagining herself in a magical garden with gossamer wings on her back, flitting from blossom to blossom. It was her favorite fantasy. But would her friends feel the same?

Suddenly, she felt nervous about the project she was about to propose. It had seemed like such a good idea when she thought of it, having her mother hire all the club members—Cricket Connors, Meg Kelly, Amy Chan, and herself—to dress up in flower petal costumes and serve hors d'oeuvres to the guests at her party next Sunday. But now Brittany wasn't so sure. Of course, if everything happened the way she hoped it would, her friends would be grateful to her—maybe for the rest of their lives. But if it didn't . . . if the whole thing came to nothing . . . But she wasn't going to think about that!

Brittany put the book back on the night table and glanced at the clock: 10:35. Now she really did have to hurry! She made a quick trip to the bathroom—her very own bathroom with blue wall-to-wall carpeting, white tiled walls, and a skylight in the ceiling—and got dressed in her T-shirt and jeans. She pulled on her socks and tennis shoes, then worked hard at brushing the tangles out of her tawny blond hair as she thought about the Always Friends Club.

The club had been started by Meg, who was also new to Redwood Grove, and Cricket after they'd discovered that their mothers had been childhood best friends. They'd had a club inspired by a book called *The Saturdays*, in which four children pooled their allowances so they'd each have more money to spend. That became the idea behind the Always Friends Club. The plan was for the club members to take turns thinking up money-making projects to carry out. After each project they'd choose one girl to spend the money they'd earned, by picking her name out of a hat.

The plan had worked fine for their first two projects. Cricket and Brittany had been the lucky ones chosen to spend the money—$100 each—that the projects had earned. Cricket had adopted a shaggy white dog named Buster and was busy spending her money on dog food and obedience classes. Brittany had spent hers on a camera with automatic focus and a zoom lens that she'd had her eye on at the Redwood Grove Camera Shop.

The trouble was, no one had figured out what to do if a project *didn't* earn money. That was what had happened with the last one—a haunted house contest that Amy had persuaded them to enter. Now Meg and Amy, who hadn't had their names picked out of the hat, felt bad. Amy wanted to earn money for sports camp next summer, and Meg desperately wanted to fly her best friend, Jenny, up from Los Angeles to Redwood Grove for Christmas vacation. All four of them had had a big argument about it last week, and even though everyone had apologized, Brittany was still upset. She hated fighting and she loved her friends and the club. If anything ever happened to them, to it . . . But she *definitely* didn't want to think about that.

Quickly, she finished brushing her hair, and took the camera she'd bought with her share of the club money from the shelf above her desk and slipped it into its case. After the argument, she'd thought that maybe she should sell it back to the camera shop and split the money with Amy and Meg. But that would have been silly. She was the official club photographer and she'd been taking pictures of all their activities for the club scrapbook. Besides, she loved the camera too much to ever part with it. No. The only thing that made sense, the only way to keep the club together, was to earn enough on this project for all of them.

Of course, Brittany knew she shouldn't get her hopes up too high. Things might not turn out the way she hoped they would. And she'd have to be careful, too, about how much she told the others. If she told them everything right away, and then it didn't work out, they might be so disappointed that they'd never forgive her!

"Brittany, are you ready?" Her mother's voice broke into her thoughts. "We'd better get started."

"I'll be right there," Brittany answered. She tucked the Flower Fairy book into the case along with her camera and then reached into her closet for a sweater. Her hand went automatically to a plain navy blue one, but then the raspberry-colored cardigan her mother had been admiring caught her eye. She took it off the hanger and slipped it over her shoulders, seeing herself reflected in the mirror on the opposite wall.

Her mother was right. The sweater did look

beautiful on her. Brittany shook out her freshly brushed hair so that it fell in shining blond waves over her shoulders. Beautiful Brittany. That's what people had been saying about her all her life. Usually she hated those words. They made her wish she was invisible. But now, for the first time, she hoped they were true. Because her entire project—maybe the fate of the whole club—depended on them!

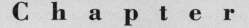

T he drive to town took about fifteen minutes down winding, tree-lined roads. Brittany liked riding in her mother's new sports car and listening to the classical music on the CD player. This time the music was Vivaldi's *Four Seasons*. Though Brittany didn't plan to admit it to her friends any more than she planned to show them her neat closet, she actually preferred classical music to popular music.

Settling back in her seat, she let the sound of the violins and horns flow over her. As it did, she found herself thinking of the *Flower Fairies of the Summer* book tucked away in her camera case. There must be books for the other seasons as well. But where were they? Probably hidden away in some dusty old bookstore or attic. Brittany wished that she had them all. With four books full of illustrations, Amy—who was probably going to declare the whole plan ridiculous—would be bound to find at least one flower outfit that she liked!

"You're sure it's going to be all right?" Brittany asked her mother. "You don't mind making the costumes? And you're not going to cancel the party?"

"Of course not!" Mrs. Logan laughed as she stopped the car in front of Elmer's Ice Cream Emporium. "Don't be such a worrywart, Brittany. The invitations have all been sent out. If you and your friends want to do it, you've got the job. Now—" She reached into her purse and took out a couple of bills. "I want you to order something healthy, like a nice tomato and avocado sandwich. Or maybe you should have an omelet since you didn't have a chance to eat breakfast." She handed the money to Brittany. "Now go on," she said, urging her out of the car. "I'll pick you up at Meg's house at around four o'clock. Have a good time."

Brittany waved as her mother pulled away from the curb. She was right. She shouldn't be such a worrywart. Everything was going to be fine. Taking a deep breath, she slung her camera case over her shoulder, pushed open the door of Elmer's, and stepped inside.

Immediately she was overwhelmed by the sounds and smells of the place—laughing voices, a jukebox playing, hamburgers cooking on the grill. Elmer's Ice

Cream Emporium was a Redwood Grove institution. Its candy-cane-striped awning, antique black-and-gold lettered sign, and the mouth-watering aroma of hot fudge that wafted out whenever the door was opened had been beckoning Redwood Grove residents for years. In fact, Elmer's had been a favorite hangout of the original Always Friends Club, and the scrapbook that Cricket's and Meg's mothers had kept was full of photographs taken there.

Their favorite booth had been at the back of the shop, and that was the one Brittany headed for now. Cricket and Amy were already there.

Amy was the first to catch sight of her. "It's about time!" she exclaimed.

"Sorry," said Brittany as she slid into the booth beside her, narrowly avoiding a collision with a waitress carrying a tray of root beer floats. She put her camera case on the table. "I overslept," she explained, studying Amy's face to see if there was any trace of resentment left over from the argument they'd had.

If there was, she couldn't find it. Amy looked the same as always. She was wearing a Redwood Grove Junior Soccer League sweatshirt paired with sweatpants—her favorite outfit—and her shiny black hair was pulled back into two ponytails fastened with sparkling blue elastic holders. On the table in front of her was a huge banana split.

"I couldn't wait," she said, seeing Brittany eyeing

the mounds of ice cream. "I was at soccer practice all morning and I'm starved."

"I couldn't wait, either," said Cricket as a waitress arrived at the table and put a cheeseburger down in front of her. "I don't have any excuse, though, except that I have to go to the dentist after this and if I get a filling I won't be able to eat for hours. You'd better order, too, Brittany," she added. "Meg's not here yet, but I'm sure she won't mind."

The smell of Cricket's cheeseburger made Brittany's stomach growl hungrily. "I'll have a tomato and avocado—No, make that a chili dog," she told the waitress. "And fries." Her mother didn't approve of fries, but what she didn't know wouldn't hurt her.

When the waitress had written down her order, Brittany turned back to Cricket. "Where *is* Meg?" she asked. "We can't have the meeting without her."

"I don't know," replied Cricket, frowning. She had curly red hair and was wearing a blue shirt covered by a vest with gold and silver buttons sewn all over it. She must have made the vest herself. Brittany thought her mother would probably admire it, if not for its workmanship, at least for its style. "She said she'd be here. But maybe she stopped at the pet shop on the way. They've got kittens in the window." Cricket loved animals and she kept a close eye on the Fur and Feathers Pet Shop. "Of course, she could still be upset about that little argument we had."

"Well, she shouldn't be," declared Amy. "I apologized. Not that I really had to. It wasn't my fault that we didn't win the haunted house contest. I did everything I could."

"Including luring Mark Sanchez to help us," teased Cricket. Mark, the cutest boy in their class, had come to their aid when they'd entered the contest—partly because he liked building haunted houses and partly because he liked Amy. "I thought he might be here," Cricket said, surveying the crowded interior of Elmer's for a glimpse of Mark's handsome face. "But maybe he's already at the high school. There's a football game today. I'll bet you're going, Amy," she added, a mischievous gleam in her eye.

Amy looked flustered. "So what if I am?" she replied. "I happen to like football."

"Sure you do," said Cricket. "Especially when Mark—"

"Cricket," Amy warned, "you'd better—"

"Stop it, you two!" Brittany interrupted before Amy could issue any threats. "No more fighting!"

"Oh, come on!" Cricket laughed. "Don't take things so seriously, Brittany. Amy and I are old friends. We're always teasing each other. Just because we had one little argument . . ."

"It wasn't so little," protested Brittany. "We all said some things that . . . what I mean is . . . well, I don't want the club to fall apart!"

"Then why don't you tell us your big plan?" said

Amy. "It's not fair to keep us guessing. You've been bragging all week about how it's going to solve all our problems."

"No I haven't . . . that is . . . well, maybe I did say . . ." Brittany tried to remember. Had she been bragging? She did recall mentioning that she had an idea for a project on the day they'd lost the contest. Maybe she had said that it was going to solve all their problems. As for keeping them guessing . . . well, she just hadn't wanted to get their hopes up.

"Come on, Brittany," Cricket urged, interrupting her thoughts. "Meg's not here, but—"

"Oh yes she is," said Amy. For Meg, wearing gray leggings and a yellow cotton sweater, had just burst into Elmer's. She was carrying a shopping bag labeled *Baylor's Children's Apparel.*

"Meg!" Amy called, standing up in the booth and waving. "Back here."

Brittany was relieved to see Meg smile as she made her way around the tables to the booth at the back.

"Sorry I'm late. But it's all your fault, Brittany," she said, sliding in beside Cricket and stowing the shopping bag under the table. "When Kevin heard I was going to see you, he insisted he was going to come with me. I had to sneak out of the house while he was in the bathroom. I didn't dare tell him you were coming over after the meeting, or he wouldn't have given my mother a moment's peace!"

Brittany blushed. Kevin was Meg's four-year-old brother and he had the most enormous crush on her. "He is awfully sweet," she said, thinking of his curly blond hair and round pink cheeks and the way he always wanted to sit beside her and hold her hand. Kevin was so cute, in fact, that she didn't even mind when he told her she was beautiful.

"Well, you wouldn't say that if you had to live with him," groaned Meg. "Anyway, when I finally got away from Kevin, my mother came running out with this shirt for me to exchange at Baylor's. I hope you won't mind stopping there on the way home, Brittany. Now what did I miss? Did you tell them your plan? Will we earn enough money for me to bring Jenny—" she began. But just then the waitress arrived to take her order.

While Meg was trying to decide between a hamburger and a hot fudge sundae, and Amy was urging her to order both, Brittany tried to collect her thoughts. All that stuff about bragging had thrown her off. She knew she had to present the project—as much of it as she was going to present, that is—calmly and carefully. First she'd tell them about her mother's party. She'd describe the garden theme and how beautiful the flower arrangements were going to be. Only after that would she mention—

"Well, Brittany?" Cricket said, as the waitress left with Meg's order. "What's the project? Tell us what you want us to be. Dog walkers? Window washers? Jugglers?"

"Flower Fairies." The words popped out of Brittany's mouth before she could stop them. It was as if they had a life of their own. She hadn't meant to say them. Not yet. But now the cat was out of the bag.

Amy wrinkled her nose. "Flower Fairies?" she echoed. Cricket looked confused.

And Meg . . . Brittany couldn't tell what she was thinking. She had the most peculiar expression on her face—almost as if she'd seen a ghost!

But there was no time to worry about Meg. Brittany had to figure out a way to take the words back. "Wait," she said quickly. "*Je n'intend pas . . .*" She lapsed into French as she often did when she got rattled. "I mean . . . I didn't intend to start out like that. I meant to tell you about the party my mother's giving next Sunday afternoon. It's going to be really beautiful, with a garden theme and lots and lots of flowers. She said she'd hire us to pass out hors d'oeuvres, and when I heard—" Brittany stopped herself just in time. She'd been about to say, "When I heard who was coming . . ." But she was not going to let *that* cat out of the bag, too!

"I mean," she continued carefully, "when I heard about all the flowers she was ordering, I got the idea that it would be even better if we dressed up in costumes to match the theme. That's when I thought of this book." She unzipped her camera case and pulled out *Flower Fairies of the Summer.*

Meg's mouth practically dropped open. "So it's

true!" she exclaimed. "That *is* what you meant. Where did you get this?" she demanded, grabbing the book from Brittany's hands.

Amy and Cricket, still looking confused, leaned over to see the picture on the cover of the book. It showed a gorgeous pink rose being embraced by a cherublike flower fairy.

"I got it in England," replied Brittany, confused now herself. She was annoyed, too. She didn't like the way Meg had grabbed the book from her hand. "In a used bookstore. It means a lot to me," she said, snatching the book back.

"Oh. Sorry," said Meg. "I didn't mean to grab it. It's just that I have all of these books!" she exclaimed.

Now it was Brittany's turn to look as if she'd seen a ghost. "You do?" she said, astonished.

"Yes." Meg nodded eagerly. "There's a *Flower Fairies of the Spring,* and of the winter, and autumn. And an alphabet book, and one called *Flower Fairies of the Wayside* and—"

"But how . . . I mean, where . . . where did you get them?"

"Well, they're not really mine," Meg explained quickly. "I found them in a big box of old books in my grandparents' attic. They belonged to my mother when she was a girl, and before that they were my grandmother's. I'll show them to you when you come over today."

Brittany could hardly believe it. To think of all those wonderful books right here in Redwood Grove. Had Meg been falling asleep at night, imagining herself in a magical garden? How incredible it would be if both of them had had the same dream!

Cricket looked impressed, too. Brittany was sure she was going to say something about kismet, which was an idea that had something to do with destiny and fate and things that were meant to be. Cricket was always talking about it.

But before she could, Amy brought them all back to reality. "Let me get this straight," she said, taking the book from Brittany's hand and leafing through the pages. "Your idea for a project is that we should get dressed up in flower costumes and parade around passing out hors d'oeuvres at your mother's party?"

"Well . . . yes," Brittany admitted, though it didn't sound so good when Amy put it that way. "Not for free, of course. My mother will pay us twenty-five dollars."

"Each?" Meg's eyes suddenly lit up. Brittany knew she was thinking of Jenny.

"Uh . . . no," she replied reluctantly. "It's twenty-five dollars for the club, all four of us. But if we look really cute, then I think that maybe . . ." Did she dare tell the rest of her plan? Meg looked so disappointed. She might be even more disappointed if—

But before Brittany could decide what to do, Cricket came to her rescue.

"I get it!" she exclaimed, looking as if a light had suddenly gone on in her brain. "Brittany, that's a great idea!"

"What is?" said Amy skeptically. The ice cream on her banana split was melting, but she didn't seem to notice.

"Her plan," Cricket replied. "Don't you see? What Brittany's trying to say is that if we look really cute dressed up as these Flower Fairies, then people who see us at the party will want to hire us for their own parties. I'll bet we could get some jobs from my mother's clients, too," she added. Cricket's mother ran a catering business and she was always supplying food for weddings and other social events. "This is a great time of year to do it, too. There are lots and lots of parties. We could probably earn two hundred dollars if we try!"

"Really?" said Amy, perking up.

"Do you think so?" Meg's spirits seemed to rise, too.

"Why not?" replied Cricket. "We can even have different kinds of costumes for different events. We could dress up as Pilgrims for Thanksgiving parties, and elves for Christmas—you know, wear red tights and hats with little bells on them. Or—But I don't mean to be stealing your project," she said suddenly, turning to Brittany. "You've probably thought of all this already."

"Oh. Uh . . . yes. I guess so," said Brittany.

The waitress arrived at just that moment with her chili dog and fries, as well as Meg's hamburger, and once again Brittany had a chance to collect her thoughts. This time there were a lot of them to collect! Everything was happening so quickly—her project was suddenly a whole business enterprise! Brittany actually hadn't thought of all the things that Cricket had suggested, but now she could see they were perfect ideas. Not that Brittany really thought they could turn this project into a business. But letting the others think they could was a great way to keep them distracted until her real plan could be put into effect. It was sort of sneaky, but—

"Brittany, you look so serious," said Meg, as the waitress left their table. "What are you thinking?"

"Oh, nothing," replied Brittany quickly. "Just that Cricket's right. It is a great idea—if I do say so myself!"

C h a p t e r

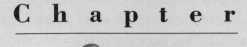

The rest of the meeting was filled with even more great ideas. Meg suggested they make business cards using her mother's computer. Amy said they could put up a notice advertising their services on the bulletin board at the exercise studio where her mother taught classes. And Cricket was certain they'd get a job right away serving appetizers for the brunch her mother was catering at the Redwood Grove Golf Club on Thanksgiving weekend. As for Brittany . . . well, it was all she could do to keep up, jotting down their ideas in the notebook that Meg, who wanted to be a writer when she grew up, always carried around with her.

She was so busy, in fact, that between talking and eating and writing she nearly forgot to take pictures. By the time she remembered, Amy had nearly finished her banana split and Meg and Cricket were on the last of their fries. She managed to get some funny shots of each of them mugging for the camera, though, and when the waitress came to clear their plates and leave the bill, Brittany got her to take a picture of all four of them.

"You'll have to take lots of shots of us in our flower costumes," said Cricket, as they slid out of the booth and headed for the cash register at the front of the shop. "Especially of Amy," she added mischievously.

This time Amy didn't rise to her teasing. She actually liked posing for pictures and she was good at it, too. All the photos Brittany had taken of her seemed to have a special kind of energy. "That's fine with me," she said. "I just hope Brittany's mother doesn't make me wear anything too icky. I'm willing to be a flower fairy if that's what I've got to do to earn money for sports camp, but no pink! Tell her I sort of like the scarlet pimpernel," she added, mentioning one of the illustrations in Brittany's Flower Fairy book.

"Well, she'll have lots more illustrations to choose from once I loan her the books from my grandparents' attic," Meg said. "Oh, this is so exciting. I can't wait to show those books to you, Brittany."

Brittany could hardly wait, either. She didn't know which she was more excited about—the project or the books in Meg's attic. As soon as they'd paid their bill, and Cricket and Amy had rushed off—Cricket to the dentist and Amy to her football game—Brittany turned to Meg. "You've got to tell me," she said as they left Elmer's and started in the direction of Baylor's Children's Apparel to return Meg's shirt. "I'm dying to know. When you look at the pictures in those books, do you ever imagine—"

"That I'm in a magical garden?" Meg finished the sentence for her. "Yes! Do you?"

Brittany nodded. So it was true! She and Meg had found the same books, and dreamed the same dream. Maybe Cricket was right about kismet. "I guess some people would think it's silly," she said, "but sometimes I feel that if I just wish hard enough I'll be able to step right into the pages of that book. Sometimes it seems as if I actually have. I can almost smell the flowers. I can practically feel the wings growing out of my back."

"I know exactly what you mean," Meg said earnestly. "Wouldn't it be wonderful if we really could do it?"

They walked on in silence for a while, Meg's shopping bag swinging between them and bumping against their legs. Brittany was thinking about Meg. Of all the girls in the club, Meg was the one she felt closest to. Maybe it was because they were both new to Redwood Grove. Or maybe it was because Meg had been the first to reach out to her, back in the days when Brittany had been acting like an awful snob—not because she was one, but because she'd been so terrified of saying or doing the wrong thing. To think that they'd been playing the same game in their heads!

"How about you and Jenny?" Brittany asked, suddenly curious. "Did the two of you play imaginary games like that?"

"Oh yes," said Meg, her face lighting up. "We made up stories together, too. Well, I made them up and then Jenny drew pictures to go with them. She's a really good artist. When we grow up, we might be a team and write and illustrate real books together. I just hope we don't drift apart like my mother and Cricket's mother did. Jenny and I write to each other all the time, but if I don't get her to come up for a visit . . ." She frowned. "Do you really think this project will work, Brittany?" she asked seriously. "Will we get as many jobs as Cricket thinks we will?"

"Well, I . . . I'm not sure," Brittany replied honestly. "But . . ." She hesitated.

"What?" said Meg.

"Oh . . . oh, nothing." Brittany bit her tongue. She was suddenly dying to tell Meg everything. It was hard keeping secrets, especially now that she'd heard how worried Meg was about staying friends with Jenny.

"How about you?" asked Meg, stepping aside as a skateboarder whizzed by them. "You must have had friends before you moved here. Weren't any of them best friends like Jenny?"

"Well, not exactly," replied Brittany. She hated to admit that she'd never had a truly best friend. "You see, we moved around so much," she explained. "Of course, there were some girls at boarding school last year who I liked. And then there was Angela. She lived in my apartment building in New York. We used to play tricks on the doorman together. And I knew a girl in Paris named Nicole. Her mother's a fashion designer like my mother is. We took riding lessons together. We would have taken fencing lessons, too, if I hadn't moved."

"Fencing? You mean with a sword?" Meg looked impressed. "Oh, Brittany, that sounds so glamorous!"

Brittany blushed. She knew that lots of things she'd done sounded that way to Meg and Cricket and Amy. But to her they were just sort of ordinary. "My mother says it's good for your posture," she explained quickly. "It's good exercise, too."

"Well, it seems pretty glamorous to me," Meg said. "I've never known anyone who—Oh look!" They were in front of the Fur and Feathers Pet Shop. "They've got kittens!"

Brittany looked into the window and instantly forgot about fencing lessons. "Oh, they're so cute!" she exclaimed. There were five of them, all slender and as active as monkeys, with sleek beige fur, big blue eyes, and chocolate-brown ears and tails.

"They're Siamese," said Meg. "Let's go in and ask if we can hold one."

Brittany could barely tear herself away from the window, where the kittens were tumbling over each other in a wild game of tag, but the idea of holding one was more than she could resist. She hurried into the shop after Meg.

The smell of dog biscuits and the call of the shiny black mynah bird who was the store's official greeter welcomed her. "Hello! Hello!" it squawked, cocking its head curiously just as the jay outside her window had done that morning.

Meg was already talking with the store owner.

"Sure you can hold one," he said. "A couple of them have already been sold. But the others are just waiting for girls like you to take them home." He reached over the partition at the back of the window, picked up one of the kittens, and handed it to Meg. Then he grabbed another one, interrupting it as it spun in circles chasing its own slender brown tail, and handed it to Brittany. "Just put them back when you're finished," he said, hurrying back to finish waiting on a customer.

The kitten felt amazingly light in Brittany's hands, not at all like Amy's solidly built, big, black cat, Midnight. With its pointed face and big dark ears, it reminded her of a statue of a cat from ancient Egypt that she'd seen once in a museum in Paris. But the cat in her hands was no statue. It whipped its tail back and forth, meowing loudly, then swatted a lock of Brittany's tawny blond hair that was hanging temptingly in front of its face.

"Hey, that's not a toy!" She laughed.

Seeming to take Brittany's exclamation as a challenge, the kitten grabbed her raspberry-colored sweater with its claws and scrambled up to sit on her shoulder. It really was more like a monkey than a cat!

Meg laughed at the surprised expression on Brittany's face. "Siamese are different from other cats," she said. "I know because my aunt has one. When I get a kitten—once my mother finds us a house of our own to live in—I'll probably choose a more ordinary kind. Maybe one from the animal shelter. These are cute, but I like fluffy cats better. Siamese are too . . ." She frowned as if she couldn't find the right word.

Brittany was sure that whatever that word was, she wouldn't agree. She didn't think the kitten sitting on her shoulder was too anything. It felt exactly right.

"You're the one who should get one of these," said Meg, giving the kitten in her hands a final tickle beneath its chin and then putting it back in the window with its brothers and sisters. "I can just picture it in your house, sliding over those polished wood floors, stretching out on that white carpet in your living room. It's definitely your kind of cat. You even look sort of alike."

"You really think so?" Brittany took the kitten off her shoulder and stared into its big blue eyes. She could feel its heart beating beneath its ribs and could count every one of its stiff white whiskers. "I've never had a cat," she said. "I've never had any kind of a pet, in fact. Not even a hamster or a canary."

"Well, you should have one," declared Meg. "You've got that big house. There'd be plenty of room.

And you could even buy it with your own money. If this business takes off, there will probably be plenty of money for everyone. Amy and I can have our turns spending it, and then you and Cricket can have yours!"

"Well, I don't know," said Brittany cautiously. "I wouldn't count on it."

"Why not?" Meg picked up the shopping bag she'd set down on the floor while she was holding the kitten. "Wait until you see the great business cards I'm going to make. In fact, you can help me. We'll start as soon as we get home—or at least after we've looked at the Flower Fairy books. But first, I've got to get this shirt back to Baylor's. Come on." Calling out a quick thank you to the pet shop owner, she headed for the door.

Brittany reluctantly returned her kitten to the window. She hated putting it down, but the kitten didn't seem to give her a second thought. It pounced on one of its littermates, then threw itself back into the game of kitten tag. Could she get one? Brittany thought as she followed Meg out the door. They were probably expensive, but if her plan for the project—her real plan—worked out . . . She hurried after Meg, thinking so hard about the kitten that she hardly noticed when they reached Baylor's.

"This will just take a minute," Meg said, breaking into her thoughts. "I'll return the shirt and choose another one really fast," she promised as they entered the store.

Baylor's Children's Apparel was another Redwood Grove institution. It had been around almost as long as Elmer's, and lots of girls from Redwood Grove Elementary bought their clothes there. Meg had gone shopping at Baylor's when she first moved from Los Angeles. That was when she'd bought the plaid flannel shirt she was exchanging today.

"It's too small for me and I'm not sure I like the plaid, either," she said, pulling the shirt out of the bag and showing it to Brittany. "My mother said I could exchange it for anything I want that's the same price, but there's so much to choose from." She gazed around the store. "Let's see . . . Oh, wait. I know!" She pointed to a colorful display set up on the girls' side of the store. "Kiki for Kids! I just love her stuff, don't you?"

Brittany's heart seemed to stop. She started to back away, afraid that she wouldn't be able to resist blurting everything out. But Meg was already pulling her toward the display, where a pair of mannequins were posed jauntily in Kiki Johnson's comfortable, fun-to-wear clothes. Behind them was a huge poster of four girls with big grins on their faces, dressed in brightly colored jumpsuits. They were lined up, with the first and third girls extending their arms and legs to look like the letter *k* and the second and fourth girls standing up straight, like the letter *i*. Beneath them were the words, *Kiki for Kids . . . of course!*

"Oh, look at that," said Meg admiringly. "They're

spelling out Kiki. Wouldn't it be fun to be a model? Especially for great clothes like these. It's a San Francisco company, I think. I wonder if—"

But Brittany could stand it no longer. "Meg," she said urgently. "Listen. I can't keep it a secret. I know that I should, but . . . there's something I've just got to tell you!"

Chapter

Brittany tried to speak in a calm and logical way, but what she was explaining wasn't exactly logical, and it wasn't something that anyone could hear and still remain calm.

Meg certainly didn't. "I can't believe it!" she exclaimed, putting her hand to her head as if what Brittany had just told her was making it spin. "You know Kiki Johnson of Kiki for Kids? She's your aunt—and she wants *us* to model for her?"

"Well, that's not exactly true," Brittany said quickly. "She's not my real aunt. I just call her that because she's such a good friend of my mother's. And she hasn't actually said . . . I mean, she doesn't actually *know* that she wants us to model for her, because she hasn't seen us yet. But she's coming to my mother's party next Sunday and when she does, I'm sure . . . I mean, I hope . . . you see, that's why the costumes are so important. Besides making us look good, they'll make us look like we all go together. What I want her to say is, 'I've absolutely got to have all four of those girls for my catalog.'"

What Brittany didn't say—what she planned never to tell Meg or any of the others—was what she thought would really be going through Kiki Johnson's mind. "Beautiful Brittany." That's what she'd be thinking. "At last I'll have a chance to get her to model for me. Even if I do have to use all of her friends as well, it'll be worth it."

But was that really what Kiki would say? Or was the whole thing just wishful thinking? Suddenly, the plan seemed incredibly risky. Maybe Aunt Kiki already had all the models she needed. Maybe even the chance of getting Brittany wouldn't be enough to make her hire Brittany's friends. And if that happened—if Aunt Kiki didn't want them—then Meg, who just a moment before hadn't thought of Kiki Johnson as anything but a name on a poster, would be terribly disappointed.

"Oh, Meg," Brittany groaned. "I probably shouldn't have told you. I don't want you to get your hopes up. There's a good chance it won't happen."

But Meg seemed not to hear. She was gazing at the girls in the Kiki for Kids poster. "Oh, Brittany, this is so wonderful!" she exclaimed. "Jenny and I used to play at being models. It was one of our favorite games. We'd dress up in our mothers' clothing and parade around the house like we were in a fashion show. There was a girl at our school who actually did work as a model. She was really beautiful, though—sort of like you. I'm so ordinary-looking that I never thought—" She stopped, finally seeming to notice the look of dismay on Brittany's face. "But don't worry," she said. "I won't be disappointed if it doesn't work out."

Brittany felt a little better when she heard that, though she didn't quite believe it. And now she had another problem. Cricket and Amy. Since she'd told Meg, did she need to tell them? She had a feeling it would be better if she didn't.

"I think we should keep this to ourselves, Meg," she said, "and not tell Cricket and Amy until later. I know we shouldn't be keeping secrets from each other, but I'm afraid that if they know before the party, none of us will be able to act naturally. I don't want us to push ourselves on Aunt Kiki. It would be a lot better if she just sort of discovers us herself. That's why I haven't even told my mother about the idea."

Meg hesitated. Brittany knew she was thinking of what would happen when Cricket and Amy found out. "Well, they'll probably be mad at us," she said finally. "But I think you're right. The more natural we are, the better. And, anyway, if we get this job, they won't be able to stay angry for long. I don't know how I'll manage it, though. I'll be so excited about meeting Kiki Johnson that I'll probably make a fool of myself. I'll bet she's really neat."

"She is," said Brittany. "Even if she is always calling me—" Brittany stopped herself just in time. She wasn't about to have any of her friends—even Meg, who was the least likely to tease her—know that she'd been called "beautiful Brittany."

"I mean, she's really great," she rushed on. "In a way, she reminds me of Cricket. She goes to flea markets and garage sales and finds old clothes that she turns into outfits for herself. And she always notices what kids on the street are wearing. I guess that's how she gets her ideas. She must be about my mother's age, because they went to school together, but somehow she seems a lot younger."

"I'm not surprised," said Meg. "Anyone who can design clothes like these . . ." She pulled a terrific-looking striped sweater off the display rack and held it in front of herself. "How would this look on me?" she asked.

"Perfect," said Brittany admiringly. Aunt Kiki really did design great clothes.

"Then I'll exchange my shirt for it," Meg declared, checking the price tag. She picked up the shopping bag and headed for the sales counter. "Then we'd better hurry home. If we want to impress Kiki Johnson, we'll have to search through those books to find just the right costumes for your mother to make."

The thought of the books erased the last bit of doubt from Brittany's mind. She was glad she'd told Meg. Now that she was in on the secret, looking through the books together would be much more fun. They could read them up in the hidden attic at the top of Meg's grandparents' house where she'd found them. Maybe her grandmother had spent the morning baking chocolate chip cookies. They could carry a plate of them up the attic stairs, then curl up on the sofa they'd made out of pillows and an old lounge chair mattress, and read and talk to their heart's content.

That was what Brittany thought. But she'd forgotten one thing. Kevin. The moment they stepped through the front door of Meg's grandparents' big old house in the redwoods, he appeared at the top of the stairs leading from the front hall to the second floor.

"Brittany!" he shouted. His face lit up with surprise. He couldn't have looked more excited if Santa Claus himself had stepped into the house. "I didn't know Brittany was coming!" he yelled, racing down the stairs.

Meg groaned.

Mrs. Kelly came into the hall from the kitchen. "Oh dear. I'm sorry," she said. "I was just about to go to the market and take Kevin with me. If only you'd been a few minutes later. Now it's going to be pretty hard to tear him away."

Brittany could see what she meant. Kevin had already grabbed her hand and was pulling her toward the family room, chattering all the while about something he'd made out of Legos. She shot a helpless glance at Meg, but she couldn't help feeling flattered at how happy Kevin was to see her. He really was awfully cute, with his pink cheeks and curly blond hair. She swung her camera case, which was dangling over her shoulder, out of the way so it wouldn't hit him in the head and let herself be dragged down the hall.

"Mom!" Meg protested, dropping her Baylor's shopping bag on the hall table. "Can't you make him leave us alone? Brittany and I want to go up to the attic to look at the Flower Fairy books."

"Well, I'll try," said Mrs. Kelly sympathetically, "but . . ."

Meg's grandmother came out of the kitchen now, too. She was holding a wooden mixing spoon, which Brittany hoped meant that she was making chocolate chip cookies. "Kevin, don't you want to go to the market?" she said encouragingly. "Your mother needs you to help her pick out the right kind of cereal."

"I don't want cereal," said Kevin. "I want Brittany."

"We could go by the pet store and talk to the mynah bird," suggested Mrs. Kelly.

"No!" declared Kevin. "I'm going to stay home."

That was too much for Meg. "Kevin, you'd better stop it!" she said angrily. "Brittany's my friend, not yours. She doesn't have time to play with your stupid old Legos."

"Now, Meg . . ." Mrs. Kelly warned.

Brittany saw Kevin's lower lip tremble. "Wait a second," she said before the tears that had welled up in his eyes at the sound of his sister's sharp words could spill over. "I know what we'll do. Kevin, how would you like me to take some pictures of you?" She knelt down and took her camera out of its case to show him. "I have just enough film left. Would you be willing to pose for me?" She knew what the answer would be. Kevin loved having his picture taken. All anyone had to do was point a camera in his direction and he was immediately all smiles and charm.

"Okay!" he said, a smile coming over his face already. "You can take pictures on the swing Grandpa built for me." He started for the back door, seeming to forget all about his mean sister and whatever it was he'd built out of Legos. But before he could open the door, Brittany stopped him.

"There's just one thing, Kevin," she said seriously, shooting a quick glance at Meg, who was still scowling. "After I take the pictures, you'll have to do an important job for me. You'll have to go downtown with your mother and leave the film to be developed at the camera shop. Do you think you can do that?"

"Of course," replied Kevin scornfully. "I'm four years old. I can do anything. Come on. Take the pictures and I'll show you." Squaring his shoulders, he opened the door and headed out to the backyard.

Mrs. Kelly was impressed. "Very clever, Brittany," she said.

"Tricky," declared Meg. "I'd never be able to get away with it. He fell for it just because he likes you so much."

"But it's not a trick," Brittany objected. She didn't like to think of herself as someone who went around tricking defenseless little boys. "I really do like to take pictures of him. He's very . . . photogenic. I think that's the word."

"That sounds like Kevin," agreed Meg's grandmother. "I just hope you don't have too much film left in your camera, Brittany, because he'll keep you out there until the entire roll is gone. You could be taking pictures for the rest of the afternoon!"

Fortunately there was no chance of that. Brittany had only six pictures left, but instead of rushing, as Meg kept urging her to do, she took her time to set up the shots carefully. She made sure that the sun was behind her and that no shadows were falling on Kevin's face.

That's what she loved about photography—looking through the view finder, composing the pictures, paying attention to the way the subject was framed. With the camera in her hands, she lost all track of time and just about everything else. And it was great having a subject like Kevin. He didn't mind posing and he could look straight into the camera without appearing the least bit self-conscious.

She took pictures of him on the rubber tire swing his grandfather had built, and on the back porch, and under his grandmother's giant rosebushes. When the film was used up, she rewound it, popped it out of the camera, and handed it to him. "Now you're going to take this straight to the camera shop, right?" she said.

"Right!" said Kevin. "Come on, Mom." He dragged his mother, who'd been waiting with a somewhat doubtful expression on her face, toward the car.

"We'll bring back the claim check for the film," said Mrs. Kelly, looking relieved. "And thanks, Brittany. You did a great job."

Even Meg was impressed. "He really was good," she said. "And it looked like you were getting some interesting shots."

"Well, we'll see," said Brittany modestly, though she was secretly pleased with the photo session, too. "You can never be sure how pictures will turn out. But Kevin is definitely photogenic."

"He is," agreed Meg, as they headed into the house, where they could smell chocolate chip cookies baking. "Maybe *he's* the one who should be a model. Too bad Kiki Johnson doesn't make clothes for little boys!"

Chapter

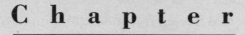

Brittany and Meg spent the rest of the afternoon in the attic, eating chocolate chip cookies and looking at the pictures in the *Flower Fairy* books. They were every bit as wonderful as Brittany had hoped they would be, and full of ideas she was sure her mother could use.

"This is going to be so terrific," said Meg, when it was nearly four o'clock and they were packing the books in a shopping bag for Brittany to take home. "How much do you think models earn?"

Brittany really wasn't sure. She just knew it was a lot. "Plenty," she said. "If Aunt Kiki hires us we'll have more than enough for everyone, plus some left over to make donations, too."

That was something they shouldn't lose sight of,

she thought. One of the goals of the Always Friends Club—besides having fun and earning money—was to help people. The girls had decided to contribute money to good causes whenever they could. They'd already given a donation to the animal shelter—helping animals was as important as helping people, Cricket had insisted—and they would have given a donation to another good cause if they'd made any money on their last project. "I think we should contribute to the Red Cross," said Brittany now. "They help a lot of people all over the world. Maybe we could give something to that group that's trying to save the rain forests, too."

"Fine with me," agreed Meg. "Just as long as we keep enough for Jenny's plane ticket and for Amy to go to sports camp and maybe for Cricket to feed Buster for another year. And don't forget about yourself, Brittany. You can't ignore a sign like this!" She picked up a paperback book from the floor and passed it to Brittany so she could drop it into the shopping bag.

Holding the book in her hands for a moment, Brittany felt the same shiver of excitement she'd felt when she'd first found it. It had been buried at the bottom of the box where the Flower Fairy books were stored, hidden beneath a dog-eared copy of *The Wizard of Oz*. The book was small and not very thick, but when she'd pulled it out of the box, the photo on the cover had leaped out at her—five blue-eyed kittens, exactly like the ones in the pet shop window. The title above the picture was *The Siamese Cat: An Owner's Handbook*.

Meg swore she'd never seen the book before. "I dug all through that box," she'd said. "I found *The Saturdays* and some other books by the same author, and a copy of *The Boxcar Children,* and some Nancy Drews. But I'm sure I never saw a book about Siamese cats. I don't know how it could have gotten there. Except maybe by magic," she'd added.

That had given both of them pause. The attic was certainly a magical place. Hidden at the top of Meg's grandparents' house, reached by a stairway that descended through a trapdoor in the back of Meg's closet, it seemed full of secrets. Even now, after the girls had straightened things up, swept away the cobwebs, and dug through boxes and old trunks looking for treasure, it still had an air of mystery and magic about it.

But Brittany didn't think magic had anything to do with the book being in the box. It had probably been there all along, stored away ages ago by some Siamese cat owner, and Meg had simply missed seeing it. But magic might explain how Brittany found the book on the very same day when the kitten from the pet store had climbed up on her shoulder and wormed its way into her heart. If that wasn't magic, she didn't know what was!

Taking a last look at the kittens on the cover, she slipped the book into her shopping bag, being careful to bury it beneath the Flower Fairy books so her mother wouldn't notice. She didn't plan to ask her for a kitten. She wasn't even going to mention the subject until she had enough money to buy one on her own. That was important. She'd tried to explain it to Meg, although Brittany wasn't really sure she understood it herself. It had something to do with wanting the kitten to be all hers—like the camera—rather than something her parents had bought because they were rich and could buy almost anything. If she got one of the kittens, she wanted to feel that she'd earned it on her own.

"Oh, I hope this will work, Meg," she said, suddenly anxious all over again about her plan. She realized now how much she was counting on it—for herself as well as for Meg and Amy and Cricket, and maybe for the Red Cross and the rain forests, too. "Do you really think it will?"

"Of course," replied Meg.

"Brittany, your mother's here," Meg's grandmother called up the stairs.

Dashing to one of the round windows at the end of the attic, Brittany peered down at the driveway to see her mother's car parked on the gravel. Voices—Mrs. Logan's and Mrs. Kelly's—floated up from the front hall.

"We have to think positively," said Meg. She

dropped the last of the Flower Fairy books into the shopping bag. "That's what Amy and Cricket would say if we could tell them about it. Now come on." She headed for the attic stairs. "Kevin's going to come looking for us any minute now."

She was right. They'd kept quiet when they heard Kevin and his mother come home from the market, but there was no keeping their whereabouts secret now. No sooner had Brittany picked up the bag full of books and set her foot on the attic stairway than she heard Kevin's voice from below.

"You were hiding!" he exclaimed. "But I found you!" After that, there was no getting rid of him until Mrs. Logan finished talking with Mrs. Kelly and she and Brittany headed out to the car.

Kevin sat down on the front porch and watched, sad-faced but resigned, as Brittany climbed into the car. He'd already given her the claim check from the camera store and made her promise that she'd show him the pictures as soon as they were ready.

"I did good, didn't I?" he shouted.

"Very good," Brittany called back, as she buckled her seat belt. "You're my favorite helper."

Meg, who was stowing the bag full of books in the space behind the front seat of the sports car, groaned. "He'll be impossible now," she said. "All he'll talk about is how he's Brittany's favorite. And he'll keep asking when he's going to see you again, too."

"Well, he won't have to wait long," said Mrs. Logan, starting the car engine. She'd arranged to come to Meg's grandparents' house after school Monday to measure the girls for their costumes. It was easier to meet there than to have everyone come to the Logan house in the hills. "And I'm so delighted to have all these books, Meg," she added as she shifted gears. "I'm sure they'll give me lots of ideas. You girls are going to be a huge success at the party."

"I hope so," said Meg. "If only Kiki Johnson—I mean—" She clapped her hand over her mouth.

Luckily, Mrs. Logan was concentrating on backing the car out of the drive and didn't seem to hear.

Meg, her face red, mouthed the word *sorry* while Brittany slid down in the seat and tried to become invisible.

"Brittany, what are you doing all scrunched down like that?" her mother asked as she turned onto the street leading into town. "And what was that Meg said? It sounded like something about Kiki."

"Uh . . . I . . . I don't know. I didn't really hear," answered Brittany, crossing her fingers.

"Well, I must have been mistaken then. After all, why would Meg mention Kiki Johnson? I guess she's just on my mind because of our lunch together. You wouldn't believe how excited she is about her new line of clothing. It's an entirely new venture for her, so . . . But I'm sure you're not interested in that. Let's talk about dinner," she said, changing the subject before Brittany—who was very interested—could object.

"Your father's away on his business trip, and it's Angela's weekend off." Angela was the Logans' housekeeper. "So what do you say we pick up some take-out food from that great deli Cricket's mother told me about, and then rent a couple of videos. We can put on our pj's and make popcorn and have a nice cozy evening watching movies, just the two of us."

Brittany could hardly believe what she was hearing. "Do you mean it?" she said, sitting up in her seat, forgetting about Kiki Johnson. She checked her mother's face to make sure she wasn't joking. Of course, what she'd suggested was just the sort of ordinary, everyday thing that most kids took for granted. But to Brittany it was as if her mother had said, "Why don't we have dinner on the moon?" They never did things like that together. There never seemed to be time. "Oh, Mother . . . I mean, Mom. That would be wonderful!" she said.

"Good," declared Mrs. Logan, smiling as if she knew exactly what was going through Brittany's mind. She turned into the shopping center where the deli and video store were located and found a parking space. "I know just what movie I want us to rent," she said. "*That Darn Cat!* It's about a cat who helps solve a mystery. Kiki told me about it today. She said it was really funny, with lots of good actors—especially the cat. It's a Siamese, I think."

Brittany caught her breath. This could *not* be a coincidence. This *had* to be magic. She looked at her mother, half-expecting to see a mystical glow surrounding her, but she looked the same as always.

"Oh, this is going to be such fun," she said, unbuckling her seat belt, not seeming to notice the expression on Brittany's face. "We'll look at the Flower Fairy books, too. We have to find just the right costume for each of you. I can see Cricket in blue, and orange for Meg, maybe yellow for you, and for Amy . . . now, let me see." She wrinkled up her forehead for a moment, then suddenly smiled. "I know!" she exclaimed. "Pink! Amy would be perfect in pink!"

Chapter

Getting through the next week wasn't easy. Besides having to convince her mother that pink was *not* the perfect color for Amy, Brittany had to resist going back to the pet shop. She was dying to hold one of the kittens again, to have it climb up on her shoulder and tickle her ear with its whiskers. But she didn't dare. Though there'd been plenty of good signs—so many, in fact, that it was hard to believe she wasn't meant to have one of the kittens—Brittany still didn't want to torture herself by wishing for something that might not come true.

"I know exactly how you feel," Meg said when Brittany told her about her decision Monday morning. They were hurrying through the crowded halls of Redwood Grove Elementary School to their classroom, having waited outside for Cricket and Amy as long as they'd dared. When it was almost time for the tardy bell to start ringing, they'd dashed up the steps and through the front door.

Where are they? Brittany wondered, forgetting about the kittens for a moment and thinking about Cricket and Amy. Could they have come in the back entrance? Maybe they were sitting at their desks in Mr. Crockett's classroom right now, wondering where Brittany and Meg were. Or maybe they're sick, she suddenly thought. Maybe they caught the same cold by taking bites from each other's lunches at Elmer's. What if they had chicken pox? She'd heard it was going around. But that would be awful! Aunt Kiki wouldn't want a couple of spotty-faced girls posing for pictures in her catalog. She turned to Meg to ask what she thought had happened, hoping she wouldn't think it was chicken pox, too. But Meg was still talking about kittens.

"If I were you I probably wouldn't go see them again, either," she said as they rounded a corner in the crowded hall. "It's so awful to be disappointed. Not that I think you will be," she added quickly. "Finding that book in my grandparents' attic and then having your mother suggest renting a video about a Siamese cat has to mean something! I think that as soon as we get the job from your Aunt Kiki you should—"

"Meg, wait!" Brittany suddenly interrupted. She

stopped in the middle of the hall. But it wasn't because she wanted a turn to talk. She'd heard . . . no, she'd *felt* something behind them. They were being followed! She whirled around just as Cricket and Amy, who'd been tiptoeing after them, burst out in giggles.

"Oh, you should see your faces," laughed Amy.

"We were waiting for you around that turn in the hall, but you were talking so hard you didn't even notice us," said Cricket. "What's up? I heard you say something about a job. Are we being hired for another party before we've even done the first?"

Brittany, who hated to lie, felt her cheeks get hot. "Uh, no . . . I mean, yes. That is, maybe," she stammered, her worries about chicken pox replaced now by another worry—keeping her plan secret.

Meg was no help. She looked even more embarrassed than Brittany. Suddenly noticing that her shoelace was coming untied, she bent down to tighten it, preventing Cricket and Amy from seeing the guilty look on her face.

But Amy wasn't fooled. "Hey, what's going on?" she demanded. "What are you two hiding? Does it have something to do with costumes? Don't tell me you've gotten us a job at a Thanksgiving party and we have to dress up as turkeys!"

"No!" said Brittany. She tugged Meg back to her feet, not about to have to deal with Cricket and Amy alone. But luckily, the idea of a bunch of turkeys serving hors d'oeuvres at a Thanksgiving party made Cricket, and then Amy, burst out in another fit of giggles. Before either of them could calm down enough to ask any more questions, the tardy bell started ringing.

"We'd better hurry," warned Cricket. "You know how Mr. Crockett feels about kids being late. We can talk about all this at lunchtime," she added.

But they didn't. Because by then, Meg had managed to pull herself together, and Brittany had decided to head off Cricket's questions before they could be asked. "I'm afraid we haven't gotten any more jobs," she explained, as they sat down on their favorite bench and opened their lunch boxes. "We just hope that we will," she said, dismissing the subject quickly, but honestly.

"We did look at all the Flower Fairy books," Meg added, following Brittany's lead and trying to steer the conversation in a safe direction. "Brittany's mother is going to come up with some terrific outfits. Imagine having our costumes made by a famous fashion designer!"

"You know, I hadn't thought of it like that," said Cricket. "To me, she's just your mother, Brittany, but to the rest of the world she's Adrienne Logan!"

"Hey, that's right," agreed Amy, looking impressed. She stopped picking raisins out of her carrot salad. "She's famous, isn't she? Probably almost as famous as that other one. You know, Cricket, the one who makes those clothes that even I like."

"You mean Kiki for Kids?" said Cricket helpfully.

Brittany didn't know what would have happened then if Meg hadn't started to choke on her sandwich and Amy hadn't leaped up and tried to perform the Heimlich maneuver—grabbing her around the waist and squeezing—while Cricket rushed to the water fountain to get her a drink. But she knew they were going to have to be super-careful for the rest of the week.

Somehow they managed to do it. It was exhausting, but by Sunday afternoon, when they gathered at Brittany's house to get dressed for the party, Brittany was sure that Cricket and Amy weren't any wiser. Especially Amy. In fact, the only thing she seemed to have on her mind—after Mrs. Logan had handed them their finished costumes and dashed off to supervise the florist who was filling the living room with bouquets of flowers—was what she'd gotten herself into.

"I can't believe that I'm doing this!" she groaned, staring at herself in the mirror in Brittany's room. The skirt of her bright yellow costume stood out stiffly above her pale green tights. "A buttercup! I just made goalie on my soccer team, and now I'm a buttercup!"

"But Amy, you look wonderful," said Brittany, not about to tell Amy how close she'd come to being a pink rambling rose. She'd persuaded her mother to make that costume for herself. She was wearing it now—a long silky pink tunic tied around the waist with ribbons—and it suited her perfectly. Her hair, which she'd washed and dried and then brushed a hundred strokes, hung over her shoulders in glistening waves, crowned by a garland of pink ribbons and roses. Looking at herself in the mirror over Amy's shoulder, Brittany couldn't help thinking that even if Aunt Kiki hadn't wanted her to model before, she would certainly want her now.

"Doesn't Amy look wonderful?" she asked Cricket and Meg. She couldn't let Amy go on sulking. Aunt Kiki was likely to walk through the door any minute, and when she did, Brittany wanted her to see all of them at their best.

"Uh . . . yes, sure," replied Cricket. She was dressed as a forget-me-not in a blue dress with a garland of blue and white blossoms in her hair. But she was too busy helping Meg adjust the wings pinned to the back of her orange poppy costume to pay much attention to Amy's complaints.

Brittany reached up to straighten her own tissue paper wings. She wished they'd had more time to practice wearing the costumes, but her mother hadn't finished them until just that morning. It had been a down-to-the-wire rush, with the doorbell ringing and flowers and food arriving while she was putting in the last stitches.

"Well, I think we all look great," said Meg, her eyes shining with excitement. She stepped away from Cricket and twirled around the room, her orange chiffon skirt billowing out and her wings staying securely in place. "This is just like a dream, isn't it?" she said. From somewhere in the house music started playing. Brittany could smell barbecued chicken wings cooking on the grill the caterers had set up on the deck.

Meg grabbed Brittany's camera from the shelf above her desk. "Take some pictures of us, Brittany," she urged, handing it to her. "We can pretend that we're models." Meg barely managed to stifle a giggle.

Brittany glanced nervously at Cricket and Amy. Meg was going to give the whole thing away if she wasn't careful. Ever since she'd arrived, she'd been dropping hints and breaking out in giggles. Brittany could see that Cricket, who had a kind of sixth sense about things, was getting suspicious.

"What's so funny about us being models?" she asked now, frowning at Meg as she adjusted her forget-me-not wreath on her curly red hair. "We'd probably be good at it."

"Not me!" Amy gave up trying to smooth down her buttercup skirt and turned away from the mirror. "I wouldn't want to be a model," she declared. "I'd never do anything so silly!"

"Silly?" Meg echoed.

"But Amy," Brittany said, suddenly alarmed. She'd always known that Amy might not want to be a Flower Fairy, but she hadn't thought she'd object to being a model. "How can you say that? You're already so good at it. Just look at these pictures of you." She put down her camera and picked up a slim picture album that was lying on her desk.

Brittany had put the album together the night before, staying up way past her bedtime, because she'd suddenly remembered that the models her mother used to advertise her clothes always had portfolios full of photographs to show. The photos were important because it was often difficult to tell, just from looking at people, how they would appear on film. Like Amy, for instance. Right now, she looked ordinary enough—even in her buttercup costume—but she shone in the photographs in the album.

"You know, Brittany, you're right," Amy said, sinking into a chair by the desk, the album spread out in front of her. "I don't know if it's me or you, but these photographs are really good." She studied the pictures of herself, then turned the pages to see the photos of the other girls.

All of them were good. Brittany had gone through every single picture she'd taken since she'd gotten her camera—two whole shoe boxes full—and selected the best. She'd even included the pictures she'd taken of Kevin in his grandparents' backyard. They didn't really belong in the album, which she'd put together to show Kiki Johnson, but they'd turned out so well she hadn't been able to resist.

"I didn't know you had so many great pictures of

us," said Meg, leaning over Amy's shoulder and being careful not to crush her wings. "I don't think I've seen half of these."

"Neither have I," said Cricket. "You made all of us look good, Brittany. Especially Kevin. He's such a pest sometimes, that I didn't realize how cute he is. Actually, we're all pretty cute," she said. "In fact, I think we look just as good as the models in that big poster at Baylor's. You know, the one that's over the display of clothes by Kiki for Kids. Why, I'll bet if she saw us—"

Meg couldn't take it. "Brittany," she said, as a car door slammed outside. "I've got to tell them!"

"Aha!" Cricket exclaimed. "I knew something was up! I could feel it!"

"Meg, no," Brittany warned. She heard the doorbell ring and her mother's welcoming voice out in the hall, followed by another voice—a very familiar voice—and then footsteps coming their way. "Don't—"

"Yes, do, Meg," interrupted Amy impatiently. "Tell!"

Meg didn't seem to notice that Brittany had suddenly moved toward the door leading to the hall. "All right," she said, her voice rising excitedly. "You're not going to believe it. But *we're* going to model for Kiki Johnson! She's coming to the party today. Brittany's got it all worked out. That's the real reason we're dressed up like this. As soon as she sees us she's going to say—"

"Model for me? What's this?"

Brittany groaned.

Meg spun around.

There, standing in the doorway, taking in every word, was a short, slim, energetic-looking woman with curly dark hair, wearing black velvet pants and a patchwork vest made out of men's silk ties.

"Oh, Aunt Kiki . . . it's . . . it's not . . ." Brittany stammered. "I mean, I'm sorry. We didn't mean to . . ."

"Don't apologize," said Kiki Johnson. She stepped into Brittany's room, gold bracelets jangling from her wrists. "If you're my new models," she added, her dark eyes flashing, "don't you think that we'd better get acquainted?"

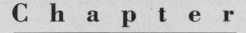

Brittany had never been so embarrassed! This wasn't the way it was supposed to happen. In her imagination she'd pictured her Aunt Kiki spotting them across the Logans' crowded living room as they flitted from guest to guest in their Flower Fairy costumes carrying trays of stuffed mushrooms and miniature quiches. In her imagination, Kiki had been so taken with them—especially Brittany in her rambling rose outfit—that she'd hired them all on the spot. Now *she'd* been put on the spot instead!

Meg's face was almost as red as Brittany's. "Oh no! Is it really you? Miss . . . or is it, Ms. . . . Kiki . . . I mean, Johnson," she stammered. "I'm so sorry. I didn't mean to say . . . we just thought that—"

"Enough!" said Kiki, holding up her hand to stop

her. "I can't stand apologies. You should never be sorry for wanting something. Even though you might not get it," she added pointedly. "But I want to see these costumes. That's why your mother sent me in here, Brittany. Turn around so I can get the full effect."

She made a circling motion, her gold bracelets jangling again. Brittany was still embarrassed, but she obeyed, turning around to show her costume. Meg did the same, followed by Cricket and Amy.

"I like your clothes, Miss Johnson," said Amy, as she finished showing off her buttercup dress. "But they're not anything like this."

"Not quite." Kiki laughed. "These costumes are lovely, of course. Just right for this party. But I don't think you could play softball or soccer in them!"

"In your clothes you can, though. I know because I've done it," Amy said. "I'm on the soccer team and I just made goalie. I don't usually go around looking like this."

"I don't, either," said Cricket. "But I am interested in clothes. I may be a designer when I grow up. If I'm not a veterinarian or a zookeeper, that is. I've got a vest that I made, with gold and silver buttons sewn all over it. But I never thought of making anything out of men's ties." She stepped forward to examine Kiki's vest more closely. "I'll bet I could get lots of them at the Goodwill store."

"That's exactly where I got these," said Kiki,

recognizing a kindred spirit. "I shop there all the time. As a matter of fact, I've gotten so many old ties that I'm thinking of upholstering a chair with them."

"A chair!" exclaimed Cricket. "Oh, that would be great. You could—"

But Brittany didn't let her continue. She was afraid that if she did, the two of them would go on trading design tips forever, and she'd never get a chance to apologize. "Aunt Kiki," she interrupted before Cricket could go on. "I really am sorry."

"I am, too," said Meg. "I never should have assumed, but I was just so excited. You see we have this club, and we're trying to earn money. I want to bring my friend Jenny up from Los Angeles for Christmas, and Amy wants to go to sports camp next summer. Cricket needs to buy lots of dog food, and Brittany wants—"

"Yes, yes, I know all about it," Kiki interrupted. "Brittany's mother told me about your club at lunch the other day. She's very impressed by the projects you've done."

Brittany was surprised. "She is? I mean, she did?" Somehow she hadn't thought of her mother talking about her when she was with her designer friends. She'd always thought that once she left the house—and in fact, a lot of the time while she was in it—all her mother thought about was business.

Kiki smiled, as if she could read Brittany's mind. "Oh yes. She talks a lot about you," she said. "She told me about the dog washing service you ran, and the haunted house. I guess that one wasn't such a success."

"It wasn't my fault, though," said Amy defensively. "It was a contest. We did our best."

"I'm sure you did," said Kiki. "But what's all this about modeling?" She looked at Brittany seriously. "I know I've sometimes talked about getting you to work for me, but usually I use professionals—kids with plenty of experience who know how to pose for the camera. It's not easy to tell who'll be good at it. My photographer and I usually hold what's called a 'go-see,' where models come in to see us. We talk to them, and look at their photographs. That part is really important. I'm afraid I can't tell, just by looking at you girls, if you would make good models. I'd have to see you on film."

"But we are on film!" exclaimed Cricket. She picked up the album that Amy had been holding and thrust it into Kiki Johnson's hands. "Brittany took these. She's a terrific photographer," she said.

"Oh, but I'm not . . ." Brittany began. She felt her cheeks get hot again. Aunt Kiki had probably worked with some of the best photographers in the world. Compared to them . . . She reached for the album, but Kiki had already opened it and sat down on the bed. Cricket, Meg, and Amy gathered around her.

From out in the hall Brittany could hear laughing and talking as the other guests started to arrive. Her mother would probably come looking for them any minute now. They were supposed to be working, after all. And from what Aunt Kiki had said about using only professional models, they were going to need the job!

"Really, Aunt Kiki, you don't have to look at that," she said, forgetting why she'd put the album together in the first place.

"Oh, but I want to," said Kiki. She looked down at the photographs of Amy that filled the first page, frowned, and then looked closer. Brittany found herself holding her breath. What was she thinking? That the pictures were awful? That Brittany didn't know the first thing about using a camera? That she had no talent for photography at all?

For what seemed like an eternity Kiki didn't say a thing. Then she looked up at Brittany. "You really took these?" she said.

"*Oui* . . . I mean, yes," Brittany replied nervously, slipping into French. She didn't know what would come next, but looking at the expression on Kiki's face, she allowed herself to hope.

"Well, they're good. Very good," the designer said. "As for you—" She turned to Amy. "There's a real spark here. You photograph very well. I wouldn't have thought it, but maybe that costume threw me off. You're really not the buttercup type!"

"I know!" Amy said. "The only good thing about this costume is that it isn't pink! But turn the page.

You've got to see Cricket. Her red hair looks great in pictures. And there are some good ones of Meg, too."

Kiki continued to look through the album, pausing every now and then to murmur things like, "Yes. Very nice. Real style there." When she reached the page full of pictures of Brittany, she stopped.

"Those probably aren't so good," said Meg. "You see, Brittany can't take pictures of herself so we have to take them for her. I always forget where the light's supposed to be coming from, and it's kind of hard getting them centered. Of course, Brittany's so beautiful, it really doesn't matter."

"Meg, don't say that!" Brittany blushed.

"But it's true," said Cricket, as Amy nodded in agreement.

"I'd have to agree," said Kiki, making Brittany blush again. "As I said, I've always wanted you to model for me. But with this new collection, what I'm really looking for—" She stopped. She'd been turning the pages of the album as she spoke and all at once her eyes opened wide. "Oh my!" she said, staring at the pictures beneath the plastic that covered the last page. "Who is this?"

Meg leaned forward. "Oh, that's just Kevin, my little brother," she said. "He loves to pose and he adores Brittany. She took those pictures the other day so he wouldn't keep pestering us. He'll do anything for her."

"Really?" Kiki looked up excitedly. "Then maybe you can get him to do me a favor. Maybe you can get him to model for me, Brittany. He's exactly what I'm looking for!"

Brittany wasn't sure that she'd heard right. "Kevin?" she said. "But Aunt Kiki, you don't make clothes for little boys."

"I do now. It's a brand-new venture for me," Kiki said. "I'm starting by designing clothes for younger boys. If they're a success I'll design for older ones. I've been having a hard time finding just the right models, but this boy. . ." She looked at the photographs of Kevin again. "He's perfect! Just look at that impish little grin. And you've captured it beautifully, Brittany. Do you think your parents would let him model for me?" she asked, turning to Meg.

"Well, I . . . I'm not sure," said Meg. "There's just my mother, and my grandparents, of course. I don't think they'd mind, and I'm sure Kevin would love it. But—" She looked desperately at Brittany, and then at Cricket and Amy.

Brittany was sure they were all thinking the same thing. What about *us*? Did we get dressed up as Flower Fairies just so Kevin could get a job? He wasn't a member of the club. He wouldn't have to share the money he earned. His mother would probably put it all into the bank for his college education. And then what would happen to Jenny? She'd never make it to

77

Redwood Grove for Christmas. Amy wouldn't get to go to sports camp. Buster would be eating table scraps for a year. And as for the Siamese kitten in the Fur and Feathers Pet Shop . . .

A vision of the kitten's chocolate-colored ears and big blue eyes flashed into Brittany's mind. She remembered its noisy meow, the way it had felt on her shoulder.

"But, Aunt Kiki, you can't hire Kevin!" she exclaimed. She was shocked by the strength of her own outburst, but she couldn't stop now. "I mean . . . we're a team. The club works together. Kevin's just . . . well, he's just sort of our mascot," she said, thinking fast. "Isn't that right?" She looked at the other girls for encouragement, but they were too surprised at the idea of Kevin being a mascot to even nod in agreement.

Brittany didn't know what to say next. Then the words—the exact right words—burst out of her mouth. "You can't have him, Aunt Kiki!" she exclaimed. "You can't have Kevin unless you take us!"

For a moment no one said a thing. The sounds of the party filtered in from the living room. Cricket, Meg, and Amy looked stunned. Brittany *felt* stunned. Had those words really come out of her mouth? She was the one who always worried about hurting people's feelings, who never wanted to get into arguments. How could she have spoken like that to Aunt Kiki?

Brittany opened her mouth, ready to take the words back if she could. But Kiki didn't give her a chance.

"Well, Brittany," she said, looking impressed rather than angry. "I didn't know you had that in you. I must say, you drive a hard bargain, and I'm not sure I can do everything you want. But here's what I can do." She paused. Everyone waited anxiously to hear what she had to say.

"If Kevin's mother is willing to let him model," Kiki continued, "the rest of you can come along. But I can't guarantee anything. My photographer will have to decide which of you she can use. If she does choose you, it will be at beginner's wages. That's sixty dollars an hour, though we may go higher for Kevin."

Amy, who was sitting on the edge of the bed, practically fell off. Meg and Cricket gasped. Brittany raced through the six times table in her head.

"I'll need to talk with all of your parents, of course," Kiki went on. "There will be some paperwork to do. And you'll have to take a day off school. We'll shoot next Thursday in Golden Gate Park in San Francisco. We've worked there before and I know we'll get some wonderful shots. There's the Conservatory of Flowers, and a merry-go-round, and the Japanese tea garden. Mounted policemen, too. We haven't had much success getting them to pose for us in the past, but maybe this time we'll be lucky."

She went on talking, but Brittany scarcely heard

what she said. They'd done it! *She'd* done it! Aunt Kiki was hiring them—or at least, almost hiring them. And not because she wanted "beautiful Brittany." No. It was because of the pictures that Brittany had taken, and because she had—how had Aunt Kiki put it?—driven a hard bargain. Brittany Logan, hard bargainer. It was the first time she'd ever thought of herself like that!

"Well?" said Kiki. "How about it? Is it a deal?"

She didn't need to ask twice.

"Yes!" exclaimed Cricket and Amy together.

"Yes!" echoed Meg.

All Brittany could do was nod.

"All right then," said Kiki, standing up. "Now, I think there's a party going on out there and I'm supposed to be a guest. I'll get all your names and phone numbers and clothes sizes later, and I'll talk to your parents this evening. I'd like to borrow this, too, if you don't mind," she added, tucking the album under her arm. "I want to show it to my photographer. She'll be thrilled about Kevin. About all of you," she added quickly. "In fact, I think our search for models for this catalog is over. We have everything we need now, except for a dog."

"A dog?" Cricket's eyes lit up. "A big shaggy dog?"

"That would be nice," said Kiki. "Preferably a light-colored one so it will show up well in pictures.

We thought it would be cute if—wait a second. You don't mean that you have one?"

Brittany laughed. "You came to the right place. This is one-stop shopping, Aunt Kiki," she said. "If you want a big shaggy white dog, you've got him."

"His name's Buster," said Meg.

"You can pay him in dog biscuits," said Cricket.

"And he's just like Kevin," added Amy. "He loves to have his picture taken!"

Chapter

An enormous pink tongue was licking Brittany's ear. "Buster!" she exclaimed, squirming out of the way in the middle seat of Amy's family's station wagon. "Stop that!" She liked dogs, especially Buster, but she wasn't about to arrive at Golden Gate Park for her very first modeling job with one whole side of her head soaking wet from dog slobber!

Cricket leaned over the seat and shoved Buster back. It wasn't as if he didn't have enough room. He had the whole rear section of the station wagon to himself. The trouble was he wanted to be sitting in the middle seat with Cricket and Brittany, or up front with Amy and her mother. He wanted to hang his head out the window as Mrs. Chan drove over the Golden Gate Bridge toward San Francisco so he could smell the sea air and bark at the other cars.

"Buster, down!" Cricket commanded firmly, as she'd learned to do in obedience class. "Lie down!"

Buster wagged his tail and stood up.

"I can see those obedience lessons have really paid off," said Mrs. Chan, glancing at the scene in the rearview mirror. "I hope he's going to behave himself today while we're at this . . . what's it called?"

"A photo shoot, Mom," prompted Amy.

"Yes. At this photo shoot today," said Mrs. Chan. "Since I'm chaperoning all of you, I feel responsible for Buster, too. I hope he'll be good."

"Oh, he will be," Cricket assured her earnestly. She'd been assuring everyone of the same thing ever since Kiki Johnson had hired Buster at the party on Sunday. "And look how nice and clean he is. I gave him a bath and brushed out his fur."

"Maybe you should have brushed his teeth, too," said Brittany. "His breath is pretty doggy. If he licks me again, I just might pass out." She was teasing. But she wouldn't have minded putting a bit more distance between herself and Buster right now. She couldn't help thinking how neat and delicate a Siamese cat was compared to a big shaggy dog!

"Well, I'm glad I'm sitting up here," said Amy. "Anyway, it's your own fault, Brittany. Dogs and little boys just love her, Mom," she explained. "It's a good thing Kevin's in the other car with Meg or none of us would have a moment's peace!"

Brittany was afraid Amy was right. Though she was sure Kevin had no more idea of what he'd be doing today than Buster did, once he'd heard that Brittany would be going along—and that there was a merry-go-round in Golden Gate Park—he'd been ready and eager to go. In fact, he'd been pestering Meg all week, and anyone else who'd listen to him, asking when the day of the photo shoot would arrive.

Everyone was excited, of course. Amy loved the idea of taking a day off from school. Cricket couldn't wait to see Kiki Johnson's new line of clothes. And Meg was more excited than any of them. She'd scarcely been able to talk about anything else since the day of the party. As soon as school was over on Monday, she'd rushed to the Redwood Grove Library and checked out a book on what it was like to be a child model. It was one of those stories with photographs that told about a real girl. There were pictures of her at go-sees like Kiki Johnson had described, and of her trying on clothes and being made up and posing for the camera.

"Isn't she beautiful?" Meg said when she showed the book to Brittany. "Look at her eyes and that wonderful hair. Actually, she looks a lot like you, Brittany. I'm not surprised that she's a model."

That made Brittany start worrying again. Meg was right. The girl in the pictures did look like her—long blond hair, slim figure, big beautiful eyes. She certainly didn't look like Meg. What would happen if Meg, who seemed to care about modeling more than any of them, didn't get chosen? Aunt Kiki had been careful not to make promises. She'd said that she'd give them a chance, but the final decision was up to her photographer. Brittany was sure she'd want to use Amy. Cricket usually photographed well, too. And as for herself . . . well, that seemed certain, especially after seeing the girl in the modeling book. But Meg . . .

She turned around in the seat, avoiding Buster's all-too-friendly tongue, and caught sight of Meg's family's car following behind them. Kevin was bouncing up and down in the backseat between his grandparents. Meg's mother was at the wheel with Meg sitting beside her. A real family outing, all of them excited at the idea of having two children in the Kiki for Kids catalog. How embarrassing it would be for Meg if—

But Brittany didn't want to think about it! She waved at Meg and Meg waved back, giving her the V for victory sign. Buster looked out the back window and barked. He wagged his tail, sweeping it across Brittany's face like an enormous dust mop.

"Oh, Buster!" Brittany put up her hands to protect herself as the tail swept her way again. She was glad she'd be riding home with her mother, who was going to meet them in the park at the end of the day. There was no way that Buster would be able to fit into Mrs.

Logan's tiny sports car!

"Well, I think it's lucky Kiki Johnson insisted on paying him in money rather than in dog biscuits," said Amy, as Mrs. Chan slowed down to pay the bridge toll before turning onto the broad avenue that led to Golden Gate Park. "He's going to need every cent he earns to pay for more obedience lessons!"

"You're right, Amy," sighed Cricket. "I guess he just didn't get it the first time around. It's expensive, though. Everything about Buster is expensive. Now let me get this straight. He gets to keep his own earnings, right?"

"Right," agreed Brittany. "That's what we decided at the meeting."

She was glad that she'd insisted they hold an emergency meeting when the party had ended on Sunday—right after they'd passed out the last hors d'oeuvres, said good-bye to the guests, and added up the number of times they'd been asked to work at other parties. "You see, I was right," Cricket had said. "We really could make a business out of this!"

No one had wanted to think of any other business but modeling, though. As soon as the meeting began, Brittany had proposed that Kevin and Buster—who weren't club members—got to keep whatever money they earned. Then Cricket had proposed that the rest of them put all their earnings from modeling into the club treasury. Meg and Amy would have first claim on it, getting $100 each to match what Cricket and Brittany had already received. Brittany suggested that they could donate some money to a good cause and divide whatever was left among the four of them.

"I think it's a fair plan," she said now, thinking of Meg. No matter who was chosen to model today, she'd still have enough money to bring Jenny from Los Angeles. "Don't you?"

"Oh yes. More than fair," said Cricket quickly. "I just wanted to be sure you hadn't changed your minds. It'll be great having Buster pay for his dog food himself. And who knows? Maybe this will be the start of something big. He could be discovered. He'd be great for one of those dog food commercials. He always gobbles up anything I put in front of him!"

Mrs. Chan laughed. "Perfect qualifications," she said, as she turned the car into Golden Gate Park. "Now keep your eyes out for that trailer." Kiki had told them they'd be shooting first at the Conservatory of Flowers, and that a house trailer they used as a changing room while on location would be parked out in front.

"There it is!" said Amy, pointing to a small white trailer parked by the curb.

"What a terrific setting," said Cricket. "I can see why Kiki chose it."

Brittany could, too. Looking out the window with her photographer's eye, she was already imagining shots. If she were setting things up, she'd have a group of girls on the lawn, playing tag among the flower beds, and maybe a couple of kids sitting on the steps playing jacks. The outrageously ornate building that was the Conservatory would be in the background.

The Conservatory of Flowers was a San Francisco landmark, the kind that appeared on postcards that visitors sent home. It was a giant Victorian-style greenhouse for plants, but its white-painted glass and gingerbread trim made it look like an enormous birthday cake. Green lawns and flower beds full of brightly colored blossoms surrounded it, making it a prime attraction for busloads of tourists. That's why they were starting the photo shoot there while it was still early. By the time the tour buses arrived, Kiki had said, they'd be done at the Conservatory and ready to move on to another location in the park.

"Look! Those must be the professional models Kiki hired," Cricket said, pointing to a group of girls wearing straw hats and colorful summer dresses. They were standing next to a raised flower bed while a bunch of grown-ups fussed around them, powdering their noses, combing their hair, measuring distances with a tape measure, and trying to erect what looked like a big white awning.

Brittany's eyes went immediately to the photographer, a slim woman wearing blue jeans and a T-shirt, her hair caught back in a ponytail. She was moving everywhere—left, right, down on her knees, up on a chair—as she tried to find the best camera angle.

Watching her, Brittany felt a sudden shiver travel down her spine. That's where I want to be, she thought. Doing something! Not just standing around getting my nose powdered and my hair combed like some kind of show dog.

She reached for her camera, which she'd stored on the floor, out of Buster's way. She'd brought it along to take pictures for the club scrapbook. She also hoped that if she wasn't too busy modeling, she'd be able to watch Kiki's photographer work and pick up a few pointers. The photographer might even say something about her photo album. That was a scary thought, but if Brittany wanted to learn, she'd have to get used to taking criticism.

"Well, this is it," announced Mrs. Chan, finding a parking space and pulling into it. She shut off the engine as Meg's mother pulled in beside them. "Everybody out!"

Cricket kept a tight hold on Buster's leash as they scrambled out of the car. Brittany held her camera and Amy carried a soccer ball that she'd brought along in case they got bored. Meg climbed out of the car beside them, followed by her mother and grandparents. Her grandmother seemed to be keeping as tight a hold on Kevin's hand as Cricket was on Buster's leash.

"Brittany, look," Meg said excitedly. "That's a

scrim." She pointed to the awning that was being erected on the lawn in front of the Conservatory. "Remember, that book explained it. It's to keep shadows from falling on the models' faces."

"Oh . . . yes, that's right," said Brittany. She hadn't mentioned it because she didn't want to sound like a know-it-all, but even before Meg had gotten the book from the library, she'd known about scrims, and a lot of other things photographers used, because she'd gone on photo shoots with her mother. The models for Adrienne Logan's clothes had been grown-ups, of course. There hadn't been any shaggy white dogs on those photo shoots, nor any little boys like Kevin, who was tugging at her sleeve right now.

"Where's the merry-go-round?" he was asking. "You said there was a merry-go-round."

"There is, Kevin," she replied. "But we can't go there right now."

"See, that's what I told you," Meg's grandmother said, coming to her rescue. "Miss Johnson said we'd go there later to have your picture taken. But now it's the girls' turn, so we have to leave them alone. We'll have a nice picnic breakfast down there on the lawn."

"That's right," Meg's grandfather chimed in. "Come on, partner. I made some nice healthy muffins." Meg's grandfather was into health food. "And we've got yogurt and strawberries. We'll get ourselves a front row seat so you can watch your friend Brittany at work."

Kevin seemed satisfied by that. He had no idea that he was the real star of the show, nor did he know what Kiki Johnson had in store for him when it was his turn to be photographed on the merry-go-round. "I see him on a pig, or maybe on one of those cute little frogs," she'd said when she was discussing her plans with the girls.

Brittany hadn't told her that Kevin probably saw himself on a tiger or a lion. And she certainly wasn't going to say anything about it to Kevin right now! To everyone's relief, he let himself be led away by his grandparents, just as a young woman strode up the slope to the sidewalk where they were gathered. She held out her hand to Mrs. Chan and then to Mrs. Kelly.

"I'm Nancy Scott," she said. "Kiki Johnson's assistant. Kiki and the art director are scouting out some other locations in the park, so I'm supposed to get you started." She smiled at the girls. "Now, don't tell me your names," she said. "Let me guess. Amy, Meg, Cricket, and Brittany." She pointed at each in turn. "Did I get it right?"

"Yes, but how—" Amy began.

"I cheated." Nancy laughed. "I saw your pictures in the photo album you gave Kiki. And this must be Buster." She reached out to pat the dog, who was straining toward her on his leash.

Brittany held her breath, expecting Buster to leap up and give Kiki's assistant a big sloppy kiss. But miraculously, he sat down and held out his paw politely.

"Will wonders never cease," said Mrs. Chan, laughing as Nancy and Buster shook hands. "But let's not press our luck." She took Buster's leash from Cricket. "We'll take him down to the lawn and set up a spectator section while you girls get ready."

"Great," said Nancy. "Keep him out of the flower beds though. We'll be using him in pictures with these girls and we don't want that nice white fur getting dirty." She turned back to the girls as the mothers left with Buster. "The clothes are in the trailer. We do makeup there, too. Not that you'll need much," she said, leading the way across the sidewalk. "You look wonderful just as you are. I'm sure you're all going to make great models."

"Do you really think so?" asked Meg anxiously.

"If it was up to me, I'd use every one of you," replied Nancy. "Now watch your step. We don't want any broken legs!" she said as she climbed into the trailer and motioned for them to follow.

Cricket and Amy bounded up the steps after her and disappeared inside. Brittany started to follow, but Meg held her back. "Brittany, wait," she said, grabbing her arm, her eyes shining. "I just wanted to thank you for setting this up. I can hardly believe it. Me, plain old Meg Kelly, a model! It's just about the most exciting thing that's ever happened to me!"

C h a p t e r

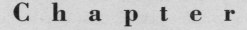

The most exciting thing that had ever happened to her? "But Meg," said Brittany, fighting a sinking feeling in the pit of her stomach, "you know what Aunt Kiki said. You shouldn't count on being chosen to model. None of us should. There's no guarantee."

"I know, I know," said Meg impatiently. "And I've been trying not to, but I can't help it. It's just so—"

"Hey, you two!" Amy interrupted, leaning out the trailer door. "You've got to get in here and see this. There's a little kitchen and a bathroom and everything. It's really neat."

"Come on," said Meg, pulling Brittany up the steps. "And stop worrying. No matter what happens, it's going to be a great day!"

Brittany wasn't so sure about that. In fact, she was

afraid that by the end of the day, Meg might not even be speaking to her, much less thanking her for setting things up!

"Brittany, what's the matter with you?" Cricket's voice broke into her thoughts as she stepped through the door. "You've got the most enormous frown on your face."

"No, I don't," said Brittany, forcing herself to smile. She glanced around the inside of the trailer. "Hey, you're right, Amy," she said quickly, before Cricket could start prying. "This *is* really neat."

And it was—but not in the sense of everything being orderly. The trailer was bursting at the seams with clothes and accessories and all kinds of photographic equipment. Brittany recognized lots of it from the shoots she'd been on with her mother. There were lights and tripods, huge rolls of colored paper that photographers sometimes used to create backdrops, and a couple of ice chests to hold the film, which had to be kept cool so the colors wouldn't change.

At one end of the trailer was a makeup table covered with all kinds of intriguing jars and tubes and brushes. A large mirror surrounded by lightbulbs was mounted on the wall above it. At the opposite end was a tiny bathroom. And right in the middle of everything was a compact kitchen with a sink and a hot plate and a small refrigerator, plus a table that folded down from the wall.

"I know it's crowded in here," said Kiki's assistant. "But this is a real home away from home. We'll be using all these clothes and most of this equipment on the shoot, and the kitchen and bathroom really come in handy when we're out on location all day. There are snacks in the cupboard above the sink and plenty of drinks in the refrigerator if you get thirsty. Now, let me show you the outfits you'll be wearing for the first shot."

Brittany stepped aside so that Nancy could edge her way to the clothes rack that was stretched across the rear of the trailer. Maybe Meg was right, she thought, feeling better. The photographer might want to use all of them. Kiki's clothes weren't just for beauties. They were for ordinary, everyday girls. And, after all, wasn't that exactly what the four of them were?

"We'll be photographing Kiki's summer collection today," Nancy explained as Brittany, Meg, Cricket, and Amy gathered around her. "We have to work on the catalog at least six months ahead, so most of these are shorts outfits and sundresses, plus some cute little jumpsuits. I think there are some great clothes here," she said enthusiastically. "Especially the things we've chosen for you girls to wear." She picked four outfits with name tags pinned on them from the rack.

"Wow! Terrific colors!" exclaimed Cricket.

Seeing the name tags pinned to the clothes erased the last bit of doubt from Brittany's mind. After all, would Aunt Kiki have gone to so much trouble choosing the right clothes if her photographer didn't plan to use them? As for the clothes themselves, Cricket was right. The colors were terrific. "They remind me of that artist who went to the South Seas," Brittany said, remembering her visits to museums in Paris and New York. "I can't recall his name, but I've seen lots of his paintings."

"Gauguin," said Nancy, looking impressed. "He was a nineteenth-century French painter. I'm not surprised that you thought of him. Kiki took a trip to Tahiti and some other tropical islands, just as he did, and I think that's where she got her inspiration. I hope these fit," she went on. "We used the sizes you gave us, and tried to choose colors and styles that would suit each of you best. Now, let's see . . ." She checked the name tag on a pair of comfortable-looking knit shorts and a rainbow-striped top and handed them to Amy. "These are for you. Kiki mentioned you liked things you can move in."

"I do," said Amy, who'd stowed her soccer ball under the kitchen table. "Maybe I can test-wear them for you when we go over to the playground later on. I think that clothes should be comfortable and last a long time," she declared. "Then you don't need to buy too many and waste a lot of time shopping."

Nancy laughed. "Well, I agree about clothes lasting, but I hope not too many girls think shopping is a waste of time, or I'll be out of a job! Now, how about these?" She held up a pair of denim shorts with bright pink suspenders and a shirt printed all over with palm leaves and hot pink hibiscus blossoms.

"Oh, that's something I'd wear," said Cricket, her eyes lighting up. "I like hot pink and I love suspenders."

"Good, because these just happen to have your name on them," said Nancy, handing her the outfit. "Meg and Brittany both get these new little jumpsuits, the same style but different fabrics." She handed a short jumpsuit of yellow cotton with a pattern of brightly colored parrots to Meg, and another in sky-blue with a pattern of white clouds to Brittany. "Any questions?"

Meg, who'd been eyeing the trays full of lipstick and rouge, spoke up. "How about makeup?" she asked eagerly. "Do we do it ourselves?"

"Not me!" exclaimed Amy, wrinkling up her nose. "I'm not wearing any of that glop! And I certainly don't know how to put it on."

"Yes, you do," said Cricket. "You put lots on your face at Halloween."

"But that was green to make me look like a witch!"

"Well, that's not quite how we want you to look today," said Nancy with a laugh. "But don't worry. You won't have to do it yourselves. We have a hairdresser and makeup man named Rick who'll take care of all that. Now, if there are no more questions, I'll leave you to get changed. You can pull that curtain closed to dress behind." She showed them a curtain that pulled across the back half of the trailer, and then headed for the door. "I'll get Rick and we'll be back shortly to do your makeup."

Meg looked like she'd died and gone to heaven. "A makeup man!" she exclaimed, the moment Kiki's assistant disappeared. "Did you hear that, Brittany?" she said. "I can't wait to tell Jenny."

Amy gave her a disgusted look. "Makeup is dumb, Meg," she commented bluntly. "He'd better not put too much of it on me! But I'm dying to try these new shorts on." She dived behind the curtain and scrambled into the shorts and top Nancy had given her. "I think they're made out of that Lycra stuff that stretches when you move," she said, bouncing out from behind the curtain and trying a few quick knee bends and kicks. "Perfect!"

"They look cute on you, too, Amy," said Cricket. "Too bad Mark's not here to see you." She ducked out of the way before Amy could send a kick in her direction. "Come on, Meg. Let's try on our outfits," she said, pulling Meg behind the curtain. "You'll have to wait, Brittany. There's not much room back here."

Brittany didn't care. While Kiki's assistant had been talking, she'd been eyeing all the photographic equipment. It made her eager to get her hands on her own camera. "Take your time," she said, slipping the camera out of its case. "I want to take some pictures for the scrapbook."

She began photographing Amy hamming it up in front of the makeup mirror. By the time Meg and Cricket were dressed she'd taken fifteen shots and almost forgotten that she was here to work as a model, not a photographer. She snapped a few more of all three girls together, then got dressed herself, finishing just as Nancy returned with a good-looking young man she introduced as Rick.

"You girls look great," he said, making all of them—even Amy—blush. "Nice features, good hair. I won't have to do much here."

To Meg's disappointment, he didn't. No false eyelashes, no fake beauty marks, no passion-pink lipstick. Just a bit of blusher brushed on their cheekbones and some cover-up for a few of Cricket's freckles. When he got to Brittany, though, he stopped, looked at her face admiringly from several different angles, and then brushed a bit of pale blue shadow onto her eyelids. "I don't usually use much makeup on kids—just enough so you don't look washed out in front of the camera. But with eyes like this, I can't resist," he explained.

"Yes," Nancy murmured, studying Brittany's face in the mirror. "Very striking." She frowned slightly as Rick finished brushing out Brittany's long golden hair. "Almost too—But we'll see what Ellen thinks," she said quickly. Turning away from the mirror, she glanced out the trailer door. "It looks like she's done with the first group. We'd better not keep her waiting."

Brittany, feeling self-conscious after all that talk about her eyes, slid off the stool in front of the makeup table. She knew Rick meant well and that he was right about the eye shadow. It did make her eyes seem bigger and bluer. But she didn't think it was how her eyes looked that was important. It was what she could do with them that counted.

Again, Brittany wished that she didn't have to go through with all this—standing around with everyone staring at her, striking a bunch of silly poses. She grabbed her camera from the makeup table. Surely she wouldn't be modeling every single second. I'll have a chance to take at least a few more pictures for the scrapbook, she thought, following Nancy and the girls out of the trailer.

The professional models, who'd been working with the photographer when Brittany and the others arrived, were straggling up the slope from the lawn toward the trailer. "Better hurry," one of them called to Nancy, dangling her straw hat from her hand. "Ellen says we're already behind schedule."

Nancy nodded. "No time for introductions then," she told the girls, herding them down the slope toward the group on the lawn. "You can meet the other models when we take a lunch break. We can't keep Ellen waiting. She's a wonderful photographer, but a real demon for keeping things on schedule."

"Oh, I hope that she'll like us," said Meg, turning

anxiously to Brittany as Kiki's assistant hurried across the lawn ahead of them. "I think we look just as good as those other girls, don't you? Of course, they're professionals, so they know what they're doing while we—"

"Meg, stop," Cricket interrupted. "It's bad enough having to pose in front of a grandstand full of people." She nodded across the lawn to where Mrs. Chan and Mrs. Kelly, Meg's grandparents, Kevin, and Buster were sitting together, waiting for the spectacle to begin. "We don't need you making us even more nervous!"

"That's right," agreed Amy. "We have to relax and try to look confident. We don't want Kevin and Buster to be the only ones who wind up in this catalog! Though I guess Brittany will be in there, too," she added. "After the way Rick went on about her eyes, she'd have to be. But at least she'll have to share her earnings with us!"

"Oh, Amy, I don't think I'm going to be the only one who's chosen," Brittany said quickly, casting a nervous glance at Meg.

"You might be," said Amy. "After all, none of the rest of us got eye shadow or—"

She was interrupted by Kiki's assistant calling, "Girls, come and meet our photographer, Ellen DeSantis."

Ellen DeSantis was the woman Brittany had

admired earlier as she moved busily around taking pictures of the models in their sundresses and hats. She was good-looking, without a trace of makeup on her face, and too busy to waste time on small talk. After Nancy had introduced them, and excused herself to hurry back to the trailer, Ellen looked thoughtfully at each girl and nodded. "Yes," she said. "Kiki was right. You girls do seem to have something. Now, what I'm going to do is take some individual pictures of you with my camera using Polaroid film that develops instantly. That way I'll be able to see in a minute how you and the clothes look on film. I'll take a group Polaroid, too, so I can see how you look together. Then, when I'm ready to start taking pictures for the catalog, I'll switch to one of my regular cameras."

She paused, regarding them seriously for a moment. "Now, I know Kiki explained that I may not be able to use all of you," she said. "I want to be sure that if you're not chosen you won't take it personally. It's not a reflection on you or how you look. My job is to take the best pictures I can for the catalog, and there are lots of things involved in that. I have to make decisions based on what's good for the work, not on what's good for you. So, no hurt feelings. Okay?"

"Don't worry," said Amy. "We can take it. We're not babies."

"Well, I just wanted to be sure," the photographer said, as Meg fidgeted nervously with a button on her parrot-covered jumpsuit. "Now, let's get started. Cricket, you first. I'd like a picture of your dog, too. He's a great-looking animal. If he's good at this, I may be able to find him more work. That is, if you're interested."

"Interested? Of course we are!" said Cricket.

Brittany could just imagine what was going through Cricket's mind—fantasies of Buster in magazines, Buster on TV, Buster gobbling his way through bowl after bowl of dog chow and kibble.

"I hope he behaves himself," Amy whispered, as Cricket rushed to retrieve Buster from Mrs. Chan, then dashed with him to the steps in front of the Conservatory where the scrim had been set up.

Brittany was less concerned about Buster than about Meg. "Don't worry," she said. "Buster's just like Kevin. He loves the camera."

It was true. Buster could be a pain sometimes, like he'd been in the car when he was licking her ear and wagging his tail across her face. But as a model he was just about perfect. He sat when the photographer asked him to, and even obeyed her command to lie down. When Ellen was done, she looked at the pictures of Buster and Cricket with a pleased expression on her face.

Amy and Meg came next, but it was more difficult to tell what the photographer thought of them. She frowned slightly as the developing images emerged on the film, then tucked the pictures into her pocket and turned immediately to Brittany. "Last one," she said, motioning her to the steps where the other girls had posed. "You're Adrienne Logan's daughter, right?" she said, looking through the lens of her camera. "You're the one who set all of this up."

"Yes," Brittany admitted. She felt her cheeks get hot. She probably looked as red as a strawberry! She would have given anything to switch places with Ellen. Brittany had left her own camera with the other photographic equipment on the lawn. If only she had it in her hands right now. If only she was taking the pictures rather than standing here blushing and making a fool out of herself in front of everyone!

"Uh . . . do you want me to smile or something?" Brittany asked, trying to recover her confidence and remembering how Amy had struck a jaunty pose, and how Cricket and Meg had smiled straight into the camera. But by the time she spoke, Ellen had already taken the picture.

Relieved that it was over, Brittany hurried down from the steps to join Cricket, who was leaning over the photographer's shoulder, watching the image develop on the Polaroid film. "Brittany's really beautiful, isn't she?" she said admiringly, as the picture of a tall, slender, blond-haired girl emerged.

"Cricket!" Brittany protested, blushing again.

But the photographer nodded. "Yes. Yes, she is,"

she said, looking at Brittany thoughtfully. Then she tucked the picture into her pocket, as if declaring the subject closed, and called out, "All right, girls, one more. Everybody back up on the steps. Just stand in a line and don't worry about posing." Before anyone had a chance to get nervous, she snapped the picture and held up her hand. "Stay right where you are for a minute," she said. "I want to see how this looks."

She leaned over the developing film as Brittany snuck a quick glance at Meg. She could see Meg was worried, and she wanted to tell her to stop biting her lip. Models shouldn't do things like that. It was bad for their makeup. But maybe it didn't matter anyway. Maybe—

"Brittany!" Ellen DeSantis looked up from the picture she'd taken. "Could you come here, please?"

"What?" Brittany snuck another glance at Meg. She had an awful feeling in her stomach, a feeling that it was over. But why was Ellen involving her? Just because she'd set things up didn't mean she wanted to be the one to break the bad news. If the photographer wasn't going to use Meg, she should tell her herself.

Brittany hurried down the steps, not daring to look at the other girls. "Miss DeSantis," she said quickly, before she could lose her nerve. "I know you're trying to do what's best, but I don't think it's fair for me to—"

"Maybe not," said the photographer, not letting her finish. "But you remember what I said. It's the work that's important. That's the way it is in this business. I'm sorry, Brittany," she said solemnly. "But I just can't use you."

Chapter

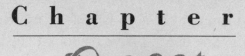

10

"**M**e? You can't use me?" Brittany wasn't sure that she'd heard right. "Are you sure you don't mean—"

Ellen shook her head. "I mean you, Brittany," she said. "I'm sorry. I was afraid this might happen after I took that individual picture of you. I thought that you might do better in the group shot, but I can see it won't work. You don't fit in, Brittany. You're just too beautiful!"

Too beautiful? Brittany's head seemed to spin. She heard the words, but she didn't know what to say. She wasn't even sure how she felt!

"What's happening?" said Meg, who'd broken away from the group on the steps and rushed over to them. "Is something wrong?"

"No . . . no," said the photographer. "It's just that I'm afraid I'm not going to be able to use Brittany for this catalog. She doesn't have the look I need. You see, I want girls all over America to be able to identify with these pictures, to see themselves in Kiki for Kids clothes. For that I need an average sort of model, like you, Meg. You have exactly the look I want. But Brittany . . ." She shook her head. "She's just not right for this job. I'm sure she could get lots of other work, though," she added quickly. "In fact, if you want to be a model, Brittany, there's no doubt in my mind you could go right to the top!"

"But I . . ." Brittany still didn't trust herself to speak. She felt suddenly free, as if Flower Fairy wings had sprouted from her back and she could fly above the lawn, over the flower beds, past the roof of the Conservatory. "Miss DeSantis," she said, her voice returning. "You don't understand. I don't want to be a model! I've *never* wanted to be a model. I hate people looking at me. I was only doing it because . . ." But she couldn't say anything more. She couldn't say that she'd been doing it because she'd thought that without her, Meg and the others wouldn't stand a chance.

Meg seemed to understand even though she hadn't said the words. "You mean you were doing it for us, Brittany. You hated the idea but you were willing to go through with it just to help me, and Amy, and the club. You were trying to keep us together, weren't you," she said. "And now . . ." Her eyes looked suddenly moist, but she pulled herself together and turned to Ellen. "You know what you should do," she said. "You should let her take pictures for the catalog. That's what she's good at."

"Really?" The photographer looked doubtful.

"Yes. Didn't you see the photo album?" said Meg, not giving Brittany a chance to object. "The one we gave to Kiki Johnson."

"Yes, but—Oh!" Ellen exclaimed. "Those were *your* pictures? I've been so frantic trying to keep everything on schedule here that I didn't even make the connection. Those pictures are very good, especially for someone your age. What kind of camera did you use?"

"This one," replied Brittany, retrieving her camera from where she'd left it. She felt dazed. How could she have been so wrong? It was Meg who was exactly right for the catalog, while she—It all seemed so upside-down! And she had to admit that though she really didn't want to be a model, she couldn't help feeling bad about being rejected—even if it was for being too beautiful!

"Excellent choice," said Ellen, examining the camera Brittany handed her. "You can do a lot with this. But how would you like to try one of these?" She picked up one of her own cameras and handed it to Brittany.

It was a beauty—the kind Brittany had only dreamed of having. Just holding it made her forget all about modeling.

The photographer smiled, as if she knew what Brittany was thinking. "I'll tell you what," she said. "If you promise not to get in the way, you can tag along and watch me work today. I'll give you a few pointers. You can use that camera, and who knows? Maybe you'll take a picture that's good enough for the catalog."

Brittany caught her breath. "Do you mean it?" she said. "Not about having a picture in the catalog. I'm sure I'm not good enough for that. But about tagging along and using this camera. Because if you do mean it, I'd love it!"

The photographer looked pleased. "Good," she said, smiling. "It's a deal. Let me show you how to use it, and then we'd all better get back to work!"

Watching Ellen DeSantis take pictures was better than anything Brittany could have imagined. Brittany had taken all kinds of lessons in her life—ballet, horseback riding, even violin—and of course she'd gone to school for years and years. But she felt that she was learning more from observing, and from listening to the comments the photographer made, than she'd ever learned about anything before.

"I don't know how it is with other things," Ellen said, "but I'm sure this is the only way to learn about photography—by watching and then trying things out for yourself. The important thing is that you love the camera. If you keep taking pictures and asking questions, you'll get better and better."

The other girls were pleased with the way things had turned out, too. Amy added up the money they'd earn with three of them working all day, and the figure was enormous, at least by Always Friends Club standards. Cricket was practically bursting with pride at the way Buster was behaving, and she was busily planning for his future career. And Meg . . . Brittany couldn't think of words that would describe how happy she looked. Instead she took some pictures that she hoped would capture it all.

The only one who wasn't happy was Kevin. Kiki Johnson had returned from scouting out locations and announced that they'd go to the merry-go-round and start shooting pictures of the little boys. The other models would meet them there. Nancy had gotten Kevin dressed in his new Kiki for Kids outfit—a comfortable cotton-knit sailor suit that looked as if it had been made for him.

But it took longer than anyone thought to pack things up. And when Kevin's grandfather, who was getting tired after watching him and Buster all morning, refused to give him a piggyback ride around the flower beds, Kevin stuck out his lip, threw the carrot he'd been eating on the ground, and kicked at the picnic basket as if he wished it were his grandfather.

Brittany saw what was happening. "Kevin," she called, dashing across the lawn, "why don't you and I go for a walk?"

At the sound of her words, Kevin's face lit up. So did his grandfather's. "Bless you, Brittany," he sighed.

"We'll just walk around the Conservatory," Brittany said. She hung Ellen's camera around her neck and took Kevin's hand. "Bring that carrot along with you," she said. "You may not want to eat it now that it's been on the ground, but there are lots of gophers living around here. Maybe we'll see one poking its head up out of a hole and you can feed it to him."

That got Kevin moving. The idea of feeding his carrot to a gopher was just about the most exciting thing he'd heard all morning. He picked up the carrot and brushed it off carefully. Then, no longer cranky, he dragged Brittany up the slope to the sidewalk.

"Don't let him get dirty," Nancy shouted, looking up from the equipment she was sorting through. "Stay on the pavement. We need pictures of him in that outfit."

"Don't worry," Brittany called back. "We'll be careful. Won't we, Kevin?"

"Of course," he replied, smiling up at her.

Looking at his round cheeks and the impish expression on his face, Brittany was reminded of why Aunt Kiki had wanted Kevin to model for her. He was going to look great in his little sailor suit with the merry-go-round horses in the background. And it made Brittany feel good that he seemed so glad to see her, even though she'd been neglecting him all morning.

She felt good, too, about having a chance to have a few moments for herself. So much had happened so quickly that she'd barely had time to sort things through in her mind. The biggest thing, of course, was that the project was a success. Though nothing had happened in quite the way she'd thought it would, Amy was going to have money for sports camp, Meg would be able to bring Jenny up from Los Angeles, and there'd still be plenty left over for donations and to share among themselves.

Brittany had talked about it with the other girls while they were taking a break. At first, she hadn't been sure that she should share in the money since she wasn't earning it. But when Amy pointed out that it had already been decided at the meeting, and Cricket commented that none of them would have gotten the job without her, and when Meg reminded her of the kittens in the Fur and Feathers Pet Shop, she'd changed her mind.

"The kittens are still there," Meg had said. "I saw them yesterday. I think you should stop on the way home today and get one. Your mother could advance you the money and you can pay her back later. If it's all right for you to have one, that is."

Brittany had no doubt that it would be all right. In

fact, ever since the evening when they'd put on their pj's and watched that video about the cat detective, Mrs. Logan had been talking about how nice it would be, now that they were settled, to have a pet. Brittany was certain that once she saw the kittens, her mother would agree that a Siamese cat was exactly what they needed.

She was thinking about the cats as she and Kevin turned a corner onto the street that led around the Conservatory. Kevin was keeping his eyes peeled for gophers. There were plenty of little mounds of dirt around holes along the edge of the sidewalk. Brittany and the other girls had actually seen a gopher earlier in the day, peeking out of a hole just like these. It had disappeared the moment it saw them, so she wasn't sure Kevin would have much success offering his carrot. But she kept her eyes down anyway, looking for a little brown head to pop up.

Brittany was staring at the ground so intently that she didn't pay attention to a familiar clip-clop sound coming their way. She didn't even look up until Kevin exclaimed, "Brittany! Horses!" He dropped her hand and almost dropped his carrot. "Look!" he cried, pointing at two mounted policemen riding their way.

For a second, Brittany was startled. She'd forgotten that there were policemen patrolling the miles of roads and trails in Golden Gate Park on horseback. But the moment she remembered, she recalled something else.

Aunt Kiki had said that she'd always wanted to get mounted policemen in her catalog photographs, but she'd never had any success. Now, here were two of them, all dressed up in their smart blue uniforms, riding their beautiful, sleek brown horses. And here was Kevin, all dressed up in his Kiki for Kids clothes, ready to pose. He even had a carrot in his hand!

What should she do? Brittany cast a quick glance back toward the lawn in front of the Conservatory. She could run and get Ellen, but that might take too long. The policemen were already riding toward a fork in the road. In a second they'd be gone. They wouldn't want to wait around while she ran off to get a photographer so they could pose for a children's fashion catalog. But they might be willing to pose for a ten-year-old girl and a starstruck—or rather a horsestruck—little boy.

"Hey, wait!" she shouted. Grabbing Kevin's hand, she ran down the sidewalk toward the policemen, Ellen's camera banging against her chest. "Could we . . . I mean . . ." She gasped breathlessly as the policemen stopped their horses and smiled down at her. "Could he feed a carrot to your horses?"

"Why, sure," said one of the policemen with a friendly grin.

"And do you mind if I take a picture?" she asked quickly.

"I don't see why not. People do it all the time," said the other policeman. "Break that carrot in half, son," he directed Kevin from his seat high in the saddle. "Hold your hand out flat. Captain, here, loves carrots. And if he gets one, old Tommy's going to want one, too." He nodded at his partner's horse, who was already eyeing Kevin's carrot hungrily.

Kevin, his eyes wide with excitement, broke the carrot in half. Brittany got Ellen's camera ready. All the practice she'd had that morning paid off. She set the focus quickly and was ready as Captain stretched out his neck and took the carrot delicately from Kevin's open palm with his soft brown lips. Brittany clicked and clicked again. She was sure she'd caught it all. The smiling policeman, the beautiful horse, and the look of delight on Kevin's face. He fed the second half of the carrot to the other horse and Brittany snapped another series of shots, getting one of Tommy reaching for the carrot, another of him taking it from Kevin's hand, and a third of the horse tossing his head while Kevin leaped back in surprise.

"You handle that camera like a professional," said one of the policemen.

"And I can see you know horses, young man," said the other.

"Did you hear that, Brittany!" Kevin exclaimed as the policemen waved and rode off down the road. "I know horses. And I fed my carrot to two of them. Mom!" he shouted, ready to race down the sidewalk. "Guess what I—"

But Brittany stopped him. "Kevin, wait," she said, grabbing his arm and looking into his eager blue eyes. "Can you keep a secret? A big secret."

"Of course I can," he said.

And he did. He didn't tell anyone—not Meg, not his mother or his grandparents, not even his favorite nursery school teacher—until Brittany said that he could. That was after she'd gotten the phone call from Aunt Kiki the following week.

The call came while she was in her room playing with her new Siamese kitten. She'd gotten him, just as Meg had suggested, from the Fur and Feathers Pet Shop on the way home Thursday. The moment she'd asked if she could get a kitten, her mother had said yes. In fact, Mrs. Logan had been almost as excited as she was. She'd insisted on buying all kinds of equipment that Brittany was sure they wouldn't need—a scratching post and sleeping basket, plus all kinds of food and cat toys.

At first, Brittany hadn't been sure which of the identical-looking kittens was the one that she'd held. But when she picked each of them up and only one meowed loudly and climbed on her shoulder, she was sure that she'd found him. She knew what his name would be, too. Monkey.

When the phone rang, she was dangling a feather, hanging from a sort of cat fishing pole that her father had made, in front of Monkey's nose. He stared at it intently, his huge blue eyes crossing slightly, every muscle in his sleek little body tense. Then he sprang, almost catching the feather before Brittany jerked it out of his reach.

"Brittany, it's for you," called Mrs. Logan, who'd picked up the phone in her study. "It's Aunt Kiki. Something about photographs."

Brittany dropped the fishing pole and dashed to the hall to pick up the extension. Her heart was racing. This was it. Would Aunt Kiki be angry, or would she say—

"Brittany! You little sneak!" Kiki's familiar voice burst out of the receiver. "Why didn't you tell us? They're wonderful!"

"They are? Do you mean it?" Brittany let out her breath. She felt as if she'd been holding it all week, ever since she'd taken the film with the pictures of Kevin and the police horses on it out of Ellen's camera and slipped it into the ice chest in the trailer along with the other rolls of film waiting to be developed. "You're not angry?"

"Angry? How could I be?" said Kiki. "You wouldn't believe how excited Ellen was when we got the film back from the lab and she saw what we had. Kevin looks wonderful! I can't wait for you to see the expression on his face. And that sailor suit. Believe me, when people see it on the cover of the catalog for my new little boys line, they're going to be flocking to the stores to buy it!"

"The cover?" Brittany gasped. "Aunt Kiki, you don't mean it."

"Of course I do. I always say what I mean," said Kiki. "Of course, we'll have to discuss payment. But that can wait. Now let me talk to your mother again. And listen," she added, just as Brittany, dazed but ecstatic, put her hand over the receiver, ready to shout to her mother. "I want to tell you something important. You're talented, Brittany. You're a very talented girl."

Had anyone ever heard such wonderful words? Brittany called for her mother to pick up the phone and then put the receiver down. She knew there'd be all sorts of explanations to come and phone calls to make—to Kevin and Meg and to the others. But right now she had to be alone. She floated into her room, scooped Monkey up from the floor, and collapsed onto her bed.

"Talented Brittany." She whispered the words into the kitten's big brown ear. He looked at her as if he knew he was hearing something significant. Not beautiful Brittany, not nice Brittany, but talented Brittany. "Yes!" she said out loud. "I like that!"

Don't miss any of the great titles in the
ALWAYS FRIENDS CLUB series:

Meg and the Secret Scrapbook
0-8167-3578-6
$2.95 U.S./$3.95 CAN.

Cricket Goes to the Dogs
0-8167-3577-8
$2.95 U.S./$3.95 CAN.

Amy's Haunted House
0-8167-3576-X
$2.95 U.S./$3.95 CAN.

Beautiful Brittany
0-8167-3575-1
$2.95 U.S./$3.95 CAN.

Watch out, Mr. Max! Here come . . .

Mice to the Rescue!

by Michelle V. Dionetti
illustrated by Carol Newsom

This engaging story features a brave
family of mice who use all their
ingenuity—plus beads, marbles, and
pincushions—to triumph over a greedy
human being.

0-8167-3515-8 • $2.50

All Don wanted was his own horse, but he ended up with a . . .

Three Dollar Mule

by Clyde Robert Bulla
illustrated by Paul Lantz

A boy's dreams of owning his own horse are nearly ruined when he buys a mule to save it from being beaten by its owner. This classic story is sure to delight young readers.

0-8167-3598-0 • $2.50

little rainbow®